LOVE'S TRIAL

BOOK 5 OF THE FIRST STREET CHURCH ROMANCES

MELISSA STORM

PARTRIDGE & PEAR PRESS
PO BOX 72
BRIGHTON, MI 48116

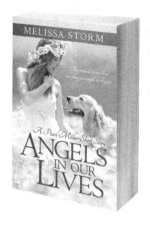

A FREE GIFT FOR YOU!

Thank you for picking up your copy of *Love's Trial*. I so hope you love it! As a thank-you, I'd like to offer you a free gift. That's right, I've written a short story that's available exclusively to my newsletter subscribers. You'll receive the free story by e-mail as soon as you sign up at www.MelStorm.com/Gift. I hope you'll enjoy both stories. Happy reading!

To Mallory.
She knows why.

PROLOGUE

Sally Scott clicked her pen, then clicked it again and again, creating a steady beat to serve as the backdrop to her thoughts. The library had cleared out a few minutes back, which meant she had a bit of precious time to herself. Well, to her story, really.

Nobody in town knew she dreamed of one day seeing her name at the top of the *New York Times* Best Sellers list, and she preferred to keep it that way. Even if her neighbors did find out about her writerly ambition, they probably wouldn't care anyway. At least not until she proved herself to the greater world first.

Before that, though, she needed to get the words onto the paper, to bring the characters to life so that one day—when she was ready—they could be shared with others. She loved escaping into her fantasy realm, a world where she made the rules and her dreams actually came true. She'd spent hours poring over both Tolkien and Shakespeare to make sure her work was grounded in not just one but two proud literary traditions.

Her hero, Benneth, made Aragorn and Oberon look like bald dwarves by comparison, with wit to rival the mischievous Puck. Yes, Benneth had everything a good hero needed, from sandy hair and striking green eyes down to a sensitive soul and willingness to travel to the ends of the earth for the one he loved.

In her novel, that lucky heroine was Salin, an intelligent scribe who worked on the kingdom's annals. Salin had fair skin, dark hair, and often found herself overlooked by the nobility and peasants alike, but she had Benneth's heart, and that was everything she needed anyway.

Okay, okay, so maybe her story had been based somewhat in her own reality. She couldn't argue that she'd used herself as a model for Salin. And Benneth? Well, he bore a few crucial resemblances to Ben Davis, the only person she'd ever loved since she first set eyes on him in kindergarten.

But Benneth had been tricked by the evil fairy enchantress in disguise, and now he was due to be wed to that same villainess known only as Solstice.

Unfortunately, that part had been based in reality, too. Sweet Grove Ben was engaged to be married to Sweet Grove Summer, and there wasn't a thing Sweet Grove Sally could do about it. Salin from the land of Lophased, though, would not be defeated so easily.

"Sally! There you are!" Ben shouted, rushing up to her large, circular desk in the center of the library.

"Well, where else would I be, Ben?" she said, delighting in the taste of his name on her tongue. "Also, we're in a library, so shhhh."

"Oh, sorry." When he smiled at her, she melted a little. So many smiles over the years, it was a small wonder Sally hadn't completely turned into a puddle at his feet.

"Hey, what's that you've got there?" he asked, reaching out to take her spiral-bound notebook, the same one that held her story. "Can I see that?"

"You most certainly cannot," she snapped.

"Oh, sorry. I didn't mean to . . ." He crimsoned. "Anyway, did you hear the news?"

The news, *ugh*. Sally had hated the news ever since Ben's fiancée Summer Smith had taken over the local paper. In fact, she actively avoided the news. It was just not fair that somehow this new neighbor had managed to win both Sally's one true love and the only paid writing gig in town. Not fair at all.

She put on a smile. She would never earn a come-from-behind victory in the race for Ben's heart if she sat here with a scowl on her face the whole day. "You seem pretty excited about it. Tell me what's going on."

He took a deep breath and then shouted again, "They did it! Jennifer and Liam actually did it!"

"Did what? And, seriously, library, remember?"

Ben continued on, only a couple of notches quieter than before. "They got married!"

"Married? What? Are you sure? Last I heard they'd gone to Disneyland for spring break."

"That's what I'm trying to tell you. They eloped, and they did it at Cinderella's castle! Can you believe it?" he asked breathlessly.

No, she honestly could not. Jennifer Elliott. Now *there* was another woman who had unfairly found her happily ever after *before* Sally—and at a fantasy castle, no less. It was like all of Sally's wishes and dreams went to God's ears, only to disappear into the ether. When would Sally's prince come? When would he realize the only one who would ever truly understand him had been right here this whole time? Had been ready and waiting for him to see that, yes, the shoe fit and she wanted to wear it?

"Anyway," Ben continued on, "Summer and I are taking the lead on planning a big reception for them. I was wondering if you could help by printing off some invitations. It wouldn't be the same without you there."

"Of course," she said aloud, mentally adding, *I'd do anything for you.*

"Great! I've still got some more errands to run, but I'll come by again in a couple of hours. See you soon?"

"I'll be here." Waiting, always waiting.

Sally watched as Ben retreated through the double doors of the old library. He was always doing that—going away, leaving her to be someplace else.

Maybe it was time Sally did that, too. Time was running out. If Ben and Summer did say "I do" come May, there would be nothing left for her in Sweet Grove.

But would she really be able to convince him that she'd been his perfect match all along?

ONE

And just like that, one wedding gave way to the next, much like Spring gave way to Summer. The cloying scent of sweet summer flowers hung thick in the air. The sun shone much too brightly, and the mass of people gathered to witness this spectacle stood too close together for any of them to be truly comfortable. That wasn't the worst of it though. Not by a long shot.

"I do," Ben said to his bride, his wife.

"I do," the imposter wearing white repeated.

Sally shifted her weight from foot to foot, trying so hard not to flee—or worse, to make a scene—as her one true love married somebody else. She glanced around the orchard. The whole town had turned out for this wedding, even though a few last-minute disasters had changed its location from some relative's garden, to the church, and finally to the old wishing well hill within Bryant Orchard.

People, she now knew, would go to any lengths to make Summer happy. Ben, on the other hand, had always been an outsider, lived on the periphery—just like Sally. At least until Summer showed up and staked her claim, stole every hope at true love right out from under Sally's poor, shaky feet.

But Sally was the hero of this story, and she refused to give up without a fight. A sea of smiling faces on either side of her watched as the Sunday School teacher, Jennifer Elliot James, led Ben and Summer through their vows.

Sally was the only one to wear a stoic expression in that moment.

Nobody else knew that the day before yesterday, Sally had at long last declared her love to Ben, had pressed her lips to his for one glorious moment forever frozen in her mind, for the only place it could maintain life, truth was in her thoughts.

Right after their brief kiss, Ben had torn away from her, declared his love for Summer, and told Sally he didn't even think they could be friends anymore. He'd ripped her heart clear in two, like it hadn't been the greatest gift she knew how to give. Like it hadn't meant anything when, in fact, her love had been everything.

Ben was the one perfect part of Sally's world. And now?

Now she had to stand in silence and watch as he became somebody else's. It was time to lay down her torch once and for all. Time to stop fighting and accept the horrible, horrible truth.

"Ladies and gentlemen of Sweet Grove," the officiant, Jennifer, said with a ridiculously huge smile on her face. It was no small wonder she and Sally had never become friends. "I now present to you, for the first time ever, Mr. and Mrs. Davis!"

Sally looked away as Ben pulled his bride into his arms for the ceremony-ending kiss. Everyone clapped and cheered. This was the soundtrack to Sally's world ending.

Laughter, joy, *torture*.

She turned to leave, but before she could, somebody flung her arms around Sally from behind. "It's been forever," her old friend, Scarlett, cried. Scarlett and Sally had gone to Sweet Grove High together, and later to college. They'd even done their master's degrees in Library Science side by side. And they hadn't seen each other since Scarlett had moved up to Anchorage and accepted a position there, leaving Sally to take over the library in their small Texas town. She'd never much cared for Sweet Grove, but at least she had Ben…

Until suddenly she didn't anymore.

All of the sudden, Summer Smith had come and changed everything.

Ruined it.

Scarlett frowned, her fair features pinched together in concern. "Sally, did you hear me? I asked how you've been. Is everything okay?"

Sally shrugged. Scarlett had known of her crush on Ben growing up, but she'd never understood how deep Sally's feelings ran. Not even Ben had known until two days ago.

Now Sally wished she would have followed in Scarlett's footsteps and taken a job in a new town, somewhere she could start over, find someone new to love. But she hadn't done that, and now she'd be forced to watch as Ben built his life with Summer as they honeymooned, became parents, grew old together.

Meanwhile she, the rather unheroic Sally, would be all alone. Forever and hopelessly alone. Some ending to this particular love story.

"You don't still…" Scarlett made eyes toward Ben and Summer standing by the wishing well on the hill. "Love him?" she mouthed soundlessly.

"I'm fine. It'll be fine," Sally answered coldly. She'd missed her friend, but she just couldn't bring herself to talk about what she was feeling today. If only there were a pill she could take… or even a surgery that could cut out the piece of her heart that belonged to Ben.

Then everything would be okay. She could heal.

But no, they didn't live in a fantasy world, although Sally spent much of her free time crafting such a land in the novel she was writing.

Scarlett placed a conciliatory hand on Sally's back and brought her in for a quick hug. "Do you want to meet Henry? He just flew in yesterday after his exams. He's studying to be a doctor, you know."

Sally did know. She and Scarlett exchanged emails often, and Sally made sure to keep up with her friend's blog even though she had very little interest in the world of dog sledding, which was the main topic of said blog.

"I'd love to meet the fire to your ice," Sally said, resigned to the fact that she'd have to stand back and watch as everyone around her found love sooner than later, while she remained with only her housebound aunt and her favorite stories to keep her company.

Scarlett giggled and gave Sally a tight squeeze. "There's the friend I know and love. And, actually, it was the other way around. I'm the fire."

Although people often called Sally an ice queen when they thought she couldn't hear, Sally knew that she, too, was made of fire.

Flames of passion, of longing, of love.

Because if she were ice than maybe—just maybe—her heart wouldn't hurt so bad.

Tobias Lloyd missed most of the ceremony, but he'd shown up just in time to watch as the groom swept his new bride into his arms and gave her that first enthusiastic kiss of marriage.

"C'mon, don't dilly-dally!" Mabel grumbled as she and the proprietor of Fred's Pizza Co. worked to unfold long plastic tables on the grass nearby.

"You're making me do ninety-nine percent of the lifting!" Fred shot back, squinting into the sun with a pained expression.

Kristina Rose and Jeffrey, the engaged couple that ran the local diner since Mabel had "retired," rushed across the lawn with heaping armfuls of tablecloths, plates, cutlery, and basically all the fixings for this triple-catered wedding reception picnic.

"Can I help?" Tobias offered, but Mabel just rolled her eyes.

"I doubt Ernie would like that," Kristina Rose said with a pout. "Anyway, we'll manage just fine."

Sure enough, Tobias's grandfather appeared behind him, pushing a polished metal cart across the bumpy ground. "Get over here, *kleiner.* We're setting up our own station on this side."

So at the end of the day, Tobias had driven more than two hours to help his grandfather further tarnish his relationship with the other restaurants in town? What a perfect reason to miss study group.

Tobias grabbed for the cart, but the old man was too quick and too stubborn to hand over control. "Gramps, couldn't we set up beside the others?"

His grandfather laughed at this suggestion. "We're the only gourmet setup in town for a reason, you know. And I don't want their fumes mixing with ours."

Tobias shrugged and tried to shoot the others an apologetic look, but they were too caught up in their own preparations. He'd never known Kristina Rose and Jeffrey well since they'd been a couple years ahead of him in school growing up, but he liked to think they could have been good friends. Maybe they still could be.

After all, he'd need friends if he decided to return to town after his law school graduation this summer. It wouldn't be long now.

He ran his hands through his dark hair, which was long only because he hadn't found the time to cut it between studying hard during the week and helping his grandfather with the restaurant whenever he had even a moment's time to spare. Perhaps he could go say hello while his grandpa fiddled with their setup.

"Where do you think you're going? I need you at the carving station," Gramps said, pushing a heat lamp into Tobias's chest.

Well, so much for laying the groundwork for a friendship. Gramps would make sure that nobody in the Sweet Grove restaurant business liked either of them, and somehow he doubted things would be different when he finally convinced the old man to hire a full-time staffer to help with the daily goings-on at Ernie's.

Tobias could wonder and worry about what came next, or he could buckle down and focus on work. Work won out every time, and it did that day as well.

It wasn't long before he had a beautiful carving station set out before him, complete with German meatloaf, pork roast, and the special red wine sauce that had made his grandpa's restaurant a local legend. Gramps had even forced him to put on a white chef's coat and hat as a further way of differentiating Ernie's fare from that of the lesser area restaurants.

That was his grandpa—passionate, particular, and proud—and Tobias couldn't help but love him for it.

Grandfather and grandson watched side by side as the receiving line on the hill dwindled. Soon the wedding and all its myriad guests would turn their attention toward the reception and the restaurateurs waiting to serve up all their best dishes.

Tobias liked being able to help his grandfather, but sometimes he wished he could just attend local events as a guest, as himself rather than as a representative of their establishment. Maybe when he was a respected attorney, complete with diploma in hand... Maybe then he could be a part of the festivities instead of a mere stander-by.

The guests continued to mill around the meadow in one giant, pulsing throng. Tobias watched and waited, trying to mentally calculate what time he could be back in Houston if he left now... or now... or maybe now. As he struggled to work out the math, a pale figure broke out from the group, her feet flying quickly over the trampled grass.

He thought he recognized her as Sally Scott, a girl who had also been two years ahead of him in school. And he knew for sure it was her when she opened her mouth to show off the gap in the center of her otherwise perfect smile.

Only she wasn't smiling. In fact, she looked as if she might burst into tears at any moment.

"Hey!" he called out, his voice hoarse and throat scratchy. When she paused and glanced over at him, he gestured for her to come over with a tilt of his head and his best smile.

"You look like you could use a good hunk of meat." He grabbed his long silver fork and began to carve a bit from the pork tenderloin laid out before him.

"Is that a pickup line?" she asked with a sniff and a scowl. "Because if it is, it's disgusting, and I'm offended."

Of course, Tobias realized only then that his invitation to eat could have easily been construed as an invite to engage in other base desires. Heat rose up his neck and into his cheeks. If she noticed his sudden blush, he could blame it on the hot lamp casting warm light between them.

Sally continued to glower at him, waiting for some kind of response to the question he had hoped was rhetorical.

Tobias fumbled for any words that could make this exchange better. "I just meant you look sad or weak or sick or hungry. I don't know." Umm, maybe he chose the wrong ones.

"So now you're saying I look ill?" She lifted one thin brow at him and crossed her arms. Her mouth closed in a frown, hiding her beautiful imperfection.

"*Oops.* Look. All I'm saying is…" He picked up his carving fork again and gestured toward the beautiful hunk of meat on the table. "I want to feed you."

"Because I'm too skinny?" Sally stood in place,

unflinching in her silent judgment. It made Tobias nervous. Real nervous.

"No. *Ahh*, no! Because it's delicious. Here." Without thinking twice, he picked up a bite-sized piece of the roast and pushed it past her lips and into her mouth.

Sally's eyes grew wide, and he watched as she reluctantly chewed the meat. He knew that the moment she was able to swallow, he'd be receiving an earful.

Not good.

Was it too late to tell Gramps he couldn't help with the reception?

TWO

Sally knew she shouldn't have stopped when the strangely familiar man at the chef's station called out to her. She was already in a far too delicate state from watching Ben and Summer tie the knot, and the last thing she needed was to make small talk with some guy she scarcely recognized from her school days.

Even though Sweet Grove was a small town, she didn't get out and around it much.

And neither did he, it seemed, or she would have at least known his name.

You look like you could use a good hunk of meat, he'd said. *You look sick, tired, sad, hungry. You're nothing next to Summer, which is why Ben chose her and discarded you like an old T-shirt—comfortable, but not something you want to let others see you wearing.*

His attempts at whatever it was he meant to accomplish mixed together with her own inner critic rose her sadness to a fever pitch. She'd just about had enough when he actually had the audacity to shove a slab of meat right into her mouth!

Now as she chewed it, appreciating the savory flavor despite her anger, she knew she was equally likely to scream and slap him as she was to turn around and run away without saying another word more.

The nerve!

So what if she was skinny, pale, and had a permanent resting *witch* face? So what if she wore her broken heart on a sleeve? That didn't give him—*or anybody*—the right to intrude on her space like that.

"I am so sorry!" he said, putting both hands up in front of him as if prepared for her to slug him before she even had the chance to swallow. "I didn't mean to… Oh, man! I just wanted to… Sorry, sorry!"

At last she swallowed the over-sized bite and could speak. "Shut up, please."

"I'm sorry. I'm sorry. I'm really…"

"Sorry? Yeah, you mentioned it. Now can you stop making a scene?" She cast a frantic glance over her shoulder, only to find that no one was paying any attention to either of them.

"Yeah, I didn't mean to embarrass you or to

assault you with my meat, or—*oh gosh!* I did it again. I…" His words trailed off, leaving a garishly bright red face behind.

She raised a finger to her lips in her classic old school librarian pose. "Hush. Stop apologizing. Stop mentioning *meat*. Just stop. You're only making it worse."

He ran his fingers across his lips in a zipping gesture and stared out at her with big green eyes that suggested he, too, was fighting back tears now. That was when she noticed.

She still didn't know his name, but she knew his eyes.

They looked so much like Ben's. Only these eyes weren't filled with indignation after she'd tried to kiss their owner. These eyes didn't betray any disgust, contempt, or derision. No, these eyes held apologies. Friendliness, even.

She could get lost in those eyes.

Sally shook her head in an effort to regain her composure. "What's your name?" she asked, shifting her gaze to his hands.

"What? I…" He ducked his head in a subtle bow, then brought his eyes up in search of hers again. "I'm Tobias Lloyd. And you're Sally. Sally Scott, right?"

She nodded, glancing quickly behind her to make sure they hadn't become the focus of the guests after the whole forced meat and muttered apologies incident. Luckily, everyone remained transfixed at the couple by the well, which meant Sally had a few moments before she really needed to disappear.

She couldn't handle the thought of Ben finding her and telling her to go away. The look of contempt that would be in his eyes, but these eyes, these eyes looking into hers now... maybe she could make them smile. Remember that, pretend they'd been Ben's, that this had been their true and actual goodbye.

"You knew me, but I didn't know you," she said slowly. She'd never been one to mince words. "Why?"

"You were a senior when I was a sophomore. And I recognized the..." He pointed toward his mouth as if to indicate the gap within hers.

Sally frowned. "You know, it's really not good form to point out people's flaws like that."

He turned redder still. She watched it happen in slow motion. One moment he was medium well, and the next he'd turned full-on rare. "I didn't mean... I meant... Actually, it's not a flaw. It's beautiful."

"Beautiful?" she asked again, focusing intently on his emerald eyes.

"Beautiful," he whispered before looking away. "I'm sure it won't be long before I'm called in to cater your wedding. Only I promise not to do the thing with the meats again that day."

"No." Now he had her laughing. The ice in her heart cracked, but it didn't melt. Not yet. "You've got it all wrong. There's never going to be a wedding to cater. Not for me."

Tobias looked confused, but broke out in an awkward, apologetic smile all the same. "Always the bridesmaid, never the bride, huh?"

"No, not even a bridesmaid. They don't like me." She motioned back toward the crowd of guests across the way. "Actually, I'm not even really supposed to be here, so pretend you didn't see me, okay?"

"Wait," Tobias called after her, but as much as she might like to stay and see how he'd manage to embarrass himself next, Sally knew it would only be a matter of time before this friendly near stranger figured out what everyone else in town already knew.

That Sally Scott wasn't worth admiring.

She was hardly even worth knowing.

Tobias watched as Sally stalked across the orchard and out of sight. What a woman she was, and what an idiot he'd been!

As an almost-lawyer, he rarely found himself tongue-tied and still didn't know why he'd struggled so much during their exchange. Sure, she was beautiful in a classic yet quirky way, and—yeah—her intelligence obviously rivaled his own, but to turn him into a stuttering moron? Now that was something else.

Sally said nobody in town liked her, and he had a hard time believing it. Then again, people often took a liking to Tobias, but it was difficult to accept their admiration when he just couldn't understand its basis.

Oh, there he went again, trotting out his mommy issues as if they explained everything that ever went wrong in his life. And yet how could he not when he wasn't even supposed to have been born?

Anna Lloyd had once had a blindly bright future before her. As the only daughter of German immigrants, a straight A student, and homecoming queen, it seemed the entire world would one day be her oyster. That is, until little, toddling Tobias came along and ruined everything.

During spring break her junior year of high school, his mother had taken a few too many drinks and a few too many liberties with a handsome stranger in Cancun where she'd gone for her vacation. Three months later, she found out she was pregnant, and three days after that, she'd made the decision to abort it—to abort *him*.

But Grandpa Ernie found out and stopped the procedure. Her parents homeschooled her until graduation so they could add learning how to be a mother to her curriculum.

Only Anna had never wanted to be a mother, especially so young. Everyone had assured her she'd love the baby once it came, that even if she didn't want the pregnancy, she would want the child. But when Tobias came, she took one look at him and knew she could never love him.

How did he know this?

Because she told him so on his seventh birthday to explain why she had to leave. She told him everything, again and again coming back to the fact that she had never asked for him, and thus the two of them just weren't good for each other.

So Anna moved out of her parents' house, and Tobias stayed behind. For all the love and affection his mother withheld, his grandparents gave him theirs in spades. But the damage to Tobias's self-esteem had already been done. He never gave up trying, though, to be worthy of her even though—rationally—he knew it was she who was unworthy of him.

He mailed her copies of his straight A report cards, sent drawings he'd made of the two of them together and happy, taped video recordings of his school plays and band recitals. She rarely wrote back, and she never came for a visit.

Eventually, Tobias stopped trying to earn her love

and shifted his focus toward proving he wouldn't be a life wasted.

Someone had saved him for a reason—God, his grandparents, he didn't know. But he was here now, and he intended to make something of himself.

Some way.

Somehow.

He kept his head down, worked hard, did the right thing whenever such an opportunity presented itself. He was cool, calm, and collected on the outside, even though inside he was a weepy, insecure mess. Appearances mattered, and people often liked the image he projected—whether or not it represented the real him.

He didn't much care for the real him, so why would they?

And why—*oh, why!*—had he let that awkward, bumbling idiot out to play today of all days?

He was so close to securing his goal of finishing law school and receiving that special piece of paper that said he was worthy, that he'd earned something so few ever did. Yet when Sally strode up to his station, he'd stumbled over his words, become awkward, vulnerable. Exactly the kind of person he'd worked hard to avoid becoming.

He couldn't afford to be vulnerable, couldn't allow

any cracks to form in the surface of his carefully crafted life.

And yet...

He turned toward his grandpa who was restocking plates and napkins at the other end of their long serving table. "Gramps?"

"Yes, *kleiner*. What is it?" he responded without looking up from his task.

"What can you tell me about Sally Scott?" Seeing that most of the guests were already served and that no one was approaching their station, Tobias cut off a slice of roast for himself and lifted it to his mouth with a smile as he remembered doing the same to Sally not so long again.

His grandfather grunted, returning to his side and grabbing a small plate for himself as well. "Who?"

They chewed in silence for a few moments until Tobias swallowed his bite and said, "The girl I was talking to a little bit ago, the one with the gap in her teeth. You know her, right?"

Gramps shrugged, his eyes firmly glued to the morsel on his plate. "What? Oh, yes. I suppose I know *of* her. She mostly keeps to herself, which is a fine thing for a young lady to do, in my opinion."

Tobias wondered if his grandpa was thinking of the errant daughter who'd abandoned them both. He knew better than to ask, though.

"Do you know where she works?"

Gramps finished his first slice of roast and then carved off another, offering some to Tobias who quickly declined. His stomach had already filled to the brim with butterflies, and there wasn't space left for anything else.

"The library, I think," he said just before plopping another piece of meat onto his tongue. "But I couldn't be one-hundred percent sure. These old eyes are too tired to read much these days. Besides, the restaurant keeps me busy."

Yes, the restaurant. The reason they were here now. He decided not to press the old man further, instead choosing to focus on finishing out the event without any more random acts of meat-foolery. Hopefully, by then, Sally would be out of his mind and he could return to school without any niggling questions as to why she'd managed to get under his skin and stay there for the better part of the afternoon.

THREE

S ally headed straight home after the wedding, more than ready to put the entire affair behind her.

As expected, her aunt sat in her favorite chair by the window staring blankly out into the yard. She startled when Sally latched the door shut behind her. "Oh, it's just you," she said, slowly letting the air back out of her lungs following her initial sharp intake of breath.

"It's always just me," Sally grumbled as she kicked her shoes into the small coat closet and shoved the sliding door shut.

Aunt Fiona rose from her chair and took measured paces toward Sally. Although she was hardly middle-aged, her shoulders hunched forward, belying years of bad posture. Her eyes were rimmed with red, and her clothes were badly wrinkled. Her straight blonde hair, though, was impeccably kept. She brushed it several times per day, one hundred strokes each session. Aunt Fiona's hair was her pride and joy… even though no one ever saw it except for Sally.

"How was the wedding?" her aunt asked.

"It was a wedding," Sally snapped back, unwilling to recount the heartbreak she'd had to suffer alone and definitely unable to live through it a second time.

"Tell me about it," her aunt persisted.

Normally Sally was happy to play her part, but today she just needed a break. "If you want to know about it so bad, then why didn't you just go yourself?"

Aunt Fiona cleared her throat and shifted her gaze back toward the kitchen.

A surge of guilt swept through Sally. She'd broken the most important rule of their relationship—the rule that stated they were always to act as if their lives were normal, that they weren't supposed to address the fact that Aunt Fiona hadn't left the house in years, that she couldn't bring herself to venture past these four walls, and that Sally was to be her eyes and ears to the town.

Nothing about it was normal, but this was their life.

Aunt Fiona's agoraphobia had crept up on them slowly. She'd once been a successful realtor, had maintained a thriving social life and had even had boyfriends. All that had ended, however, when she got the call that her sister and brother-in-law had perished in a car accident and she was now the guardian of their little girl, Sally.

Sally had been five, still so young but also old enough to see that things were changing—and not for the better. It started with driving. Every time Aunt Fiona got behind the wheel of her little sedan to drive Sally to school or a playdate, she would start breathing fast and turning a bright lobster shade of red. She'd then say she was too dizzy to drive and would tell Sally to arrange to have her friends' parents pick her up the next time.

They drove so rarely that eventually Aunt Fiona sold the car, and they began walking everywhere instead. As Sally got older, her aunt had less and less of a reason to leave the home. She hadn't always been afraid, but her anxiety became reinforced by habit, and soon the world was too big a place for her to be a part of it.

Sally could still clearly remember the last time Aunt Fiona had left the house. It had been for her high school graduation more than eight years ago. She hadn't come to Sally's college ceremonies because she could neither drive such a long distance nor bring herself to board a plane.

Sally had hoped to break free once she had her degree in hand, but her aunt had retreated even further into herself during Sally's absence. She couldn't just abandon the woman now, not when she had taken little Sally in when she had no one else to love her.

And so this was Sally's world—library, home, library, home. She so badly wanted it to be different, but life was something that happened, not something you could choose. Until recently she'd foolishly allowed herself to believe she could select a different path for herself with Ben, but that had only led to the complete and utter destruction of any lingering hope that life could be better someday, somehow.

"I'm sorry. I didn't mean to snap. I'm just tired from all that time in the sun," Sally said, placing a hand gently on her aunt's shoulder before she could turn away. "It was a beautiful ceremony. They ended up holding it in the orchard at the old wishing well. Everyone threw pennies into the well to make wishes for Ben and Summer's married life."

"That sounds nice." Aunt Fiona closed her eyes, and Sally knew she was picturing the scene for herself.

Sally couldn't hold back her sudden laugh that

bubbled to the surface. "It was nice. Well, until one of the caterers assaulted me with meat."

Her aunt's eyes blinked open again, the dull browns searching for some kind of explanation in Sally's face.

She smiled to allay her aunt's fears. "It's a long story, but I'm fine. Hey, shall we make some tea and listen to another chapter or two?"

Aunt Fiona let the tension out of her body, a noticeable loosening and letting go. "That would be nice, dear. Thank you." She headed to the kitchen to prepare a pitcher of raspberry iced tea while Sally brought out the speaker and scrolled through the selections in their shared Audible account.

They'd both always been big readers. It was her aunt's way of having adventures out in the big world while remaining safely ensconced in her home, and it was Sally's way of having friends, of belonging, of being really and truly normal. Sometimes make believe was the only way to replace the things you just couldn't have. They both understood that quite well.

A few years ago they'd decided to start sharing the activity by listening to audiobooks together in the living room while Aunt Fiona worked on puzzles and Sally sat with her eyes closed and allowed the story to wash over her.

Maybe this was why she'd had no luck as a writer. She loved books and wanted to add her voice to the great literary canon, to see her name in print, to touch readers' hearts and imaginations. But she'd always used books like friends, as a way to feel normal, and now that she sat to write her own stories, she found that she didn't have the slightest idea how to go about it. She needed the stories to stay sane, but every time she opened her imagination to something new, all the pain flowed out onto the page into a hideous mess of words that no one would ever want to read.

Especially not Sally herself.

The interviewer smiled at Tobias and leaned back in his chair. The buttons of his shirt strained against the girth around his midsection, suggesting a recent weight gain. But if the man was under an undue amount of stress these days, he certainly didn't show it. "And what would you say is your greatest strength?" he asked, tapping his pen at the edge of his large cherry desk.

Tobias rattled off the same answer he'd given to every other perspective law firm employer. "My perseverance in the face of adversity," he answered with a nod, mimicking the interviewer's posture as all the job prep guides had insisted he do.

They exchanged a few more questions, answers, pleasantries, and in no time at all, the interviewer had stood and was extending his hand toward Tobias. "This went great, really great, but we still have several more interviews to conduct before making our decision. Either way, it was great to meet you, Mr. Lloyd. We'll be in touch."

Tobias shuffled out of the office, keeping his head held high in feigned confidence. He'd done so many interviews, but still he had no offers on his plate. Did that mean he was fundamentally unhireable despite graduating near the top of his class at Thurgood Marshall? And what did it mean that the interviewer had used the word *great* three times in such rapid succession? Perhaps he was just humoring Tobias. Perhaps it hadn't gone "great" at all.

Whatever the case, he needed to find some kind of job and quick. Soon there would be bills to pay, including his excessively lofty student loans. Law school was supposed to be the difficult part, not what came next.

Still, he would persevere in the face of adversity like he always had—his greatest strength wasn't just corporate speak. It was true to life, too.

As Tobias walked down the long corridor that led

back to the outside, he felt his phone buzz in his pocket. Who could it be? Someone with a job offer, he hoped.

But, no, he'd received a text from his grandfather's phone.

This is Liam James, the message read. *We were at the restaurant when your grandfather fainted, headed to hospital now. Any way you can come home for a few days?*

Tobias felt his heart drop. His grandfather was the only person in this world he truly felt close to, truly loved. He couldn't afford to lose him now... or ever, for that matter.

"Please don't be a heart attack, please don't be a heart attack," he mumbled to himself over and over again as he worked up the nerve to call Liam and demand more information.

He'd already lost his grandmother five years back. She'd always been the healthier of his two grandparents, but one day she'd had a massive heart attack and, well, that was it. There was nothing anyone could do. Tobias was studying for his midterms when his grandfather called to deliver the news, and nothing had been the same since.

Back then, Tobias had half expected his gramps to drop dead of a broken heart, too—but the old man proved too stubborn to leave the world behind just yet. Hopefully, that surliness was still flowing through his veins. Tobias could not lose him. He couldn't even think about that possibility.

Liam answered on the first ring. "Tobias," he answered breathlessly. "I was hoping you'd call back."

"How's my grandpa? Is he okay?"

"He's awake now and insisting he doesn't need the hospital."

Tobias chuckled with relief. "Sounds about right." Gramps murmured something in the background, but Tobias couldn't make it out. "What's he saying?"

"He's saying not to come. That he's fine."

"I'm already on my way," Tobias answered, shoving the key into the ignition. Maybe stubbornness was a trait that ran in their family. After all, wasn't that just another word for perseverance?

"Figured you'd say that," Liam said. "We're almost to St. Joseph's. I'll call you when we learn something more."

They said goodbye, and Tobias headed for the highway. Thoughts sped through his mind like crazed drivers, all racing to reach their destination first.

What if his grandfather was seriously ill?

What if he was going to die?

What if he wasn't?

What if Tobias got a job offer outside of Texas and

ended up moving too far to visit his grandpa on a regular basis?

Would Gramps be willing to leave Sweet Grove and his restaurant behind?

Could Tobias ask that of him?

By the time he reached the turn off for St. Joe's, Tobias had already decided.

He was coming home.

FOUR

Sally hadn't talked to Ben since his wedding nearly two months before. The library had once been her friend's favorite place, somewhere he visited almost every day. He'd stopped coming altogether now, though. On the few occasions they ran into each other around town, Ben ducked his head and disappeared before Sally could try to make conversation.

Even worse than the prolonged absence of Ben was the new ubiquity of his bride Summer in Sally's life. Now it was *she* who dropped by the library to check out books and return them a few days later. And she was always kind to Sally—unbearably so.

Surely she knew about Sally's attempts to get Ben to abandon their wedding and run away with her instead. But if she did, Summer showed no contempt in her interactions with Sally. In fact, it was pity that lingered in her expression once her smile had neutralized.

"How are you doing?" she'd ask every single time they're paths crossed.

"Fine," Sally would answer, forcing a smile of her own. She often wondered if Summer liked gloating her victory over Sally or if their rivalry only existed within her own overactive imagination.

Today Summer brought several volumes on the French Revolution to the front desk and thunked them down in front of Sally. They exchanged their usual greetings, but Summer decided to take the conversation down a new path that day. "Have you heard the news?" she asked, tipping her head up as she spoke.

"Depends on what news you're talking about," Sally answered flatly, keeping her eyes on the books as she scanned and stamped each one.

"Fred's officially thrown in the towel," Summer revealed with a quick rap at the table. "He's backed out of his lease and is already packing up to leave town. Isn't that so sad?"

Sally shrugged. She'd never liked Fred's pizza very much, and even though there were many Sweet Grove residents who did, apparently, they didn't go often enough to keep the old guy in business. Besides, it was a well-known fact that the business at Pine Boulevard turned over like crazy. Fred had made it three years, which was practically a record.

"It's what happens," Sally said. "Fred's tough. He'll be just fine."

Summer shook her head and frowned. "To think my wedding was one of the last times anyone will have ever had the chance to eat his pizza."

She studied Sally as if to make sure the barb had stung as much as possible while sinking in. "I just wish Fred would have let on how much he was struggling. If he'd told us, then Ben and I could have had him do the full job rather than splitting the budget between him, Mabel, and Ernie."

"You're all set here," Sally said, thanking her lucky stars she was so efficient at her job that she could get Summer out of there without any more ridiculous small talk, as she pushed the stack of books toward Summer, forming a barrier between the two of them. "Have a good day."

Summer frowned and looked as if she wanted to say more, but at last she picked up the books and walked away, leaving a trail of floral perfume in her wake.

Once the door swung close behind her, the library fell quiet again. The loudest sound was the humming of the fluorescent lighting that buzzed overhead. Like Fred, Sally never had too much business, either.

Thankfully, the library was a government entity and a town treasure, which meant her job would be secure as long as she needed it.

Unfortunately, there'd been mounting pressure from her boss, Mayor Matthew Bryant, as to what all the duties of her job should entail. The Mayor had suggested she assist with other tasks about town—things like the *Sweet Grove Sentinel*, the school board, and even the chamber of commerce.

But Sally was a librarian because she liked books, not out of a desire to be some kind of pinnacle in the local community. And she definitely didn't want a thing to do with the *Sentinel*, where Summer worked as the editor and lead reporter.

It was bad enough that Sally had to see her at the library a couple times per week. She'd die if she had to spend any real quality time with the woman who had stolen her life and love right out from under her nose.

Using the news of Fred's closing to lord her wedding over Sally, though, was a new low. Everyone else in town adored Summer, but Sally saw right through her. She saw the insecurities, the desperate need to please everyone—thus having hired three caterers instead of one.

Sally, on the other hand, only needed to keep herself happy. And in that way, she was freer than them all. Summer's wedding had been far too much of a production. It had been all Summer and very little Ben. The only part Sally herself enjoyed was the brief conversation she'd had with Tobias Lloyd at his carving station.

Awkward as it had been, at least it was something real in a town that felt anything but. The people were the same, so much so that sometimes she had to check to make sure she wasn't trapped in some bizarre Groundhogs Day-like time loop.

Nothing ever changed. Even Fred's going out of business represented more of the same—the same pattern, same people, same boring life.

Sally needed to find a way out before it absorbed her whole... or worse, it trapped her inside like her aunt. Small towns were great when you loved everyone and everything inside, but for Sally, Sweet Grove felt like a snow globe whose walls were slowly shrinking toward the center.

She needed to find a way to shake things up before everything closed in on her and she died of suffocation.

Tobias flew through the parking lot and into a hospital he hadn't visited since he'd broken his arm as a teenager. He found Liam waiting for him in the lobby. The other man jumped to his feet the moment he spotted Tobias.

"Thank you so much for staying with him until I got here," Tobias said, not even hesitating to hug the man who could have very well saved his Gramps's life. He would forever owe Liam a debt, and one day he would find a way to help him as Liam had helped his family.

"Well, I'm not exactly *with* him." Liam sighed and shoved both hands deep into his pockets. "They wouldn't let me back since I'm not related, but I'm here for him. *For you.*"

"Any news?" Tobias frowned upon realizing that Liam was no stranger to hospitals. He'd spent the better part of a year here as his late wife battled—and ultimately was defeated by—neurocancer. Somehow that made his willingness to help Gramps mean even more.

Tobias wondered if he should ask how Liam was doing, if he should apologize for his needing to return to a place he undoubtedly associated with such negative memories. But the other man seemed to be focused on Tobias's needs one hundred percent.

He'd surprised the entire town earlier that year by remarrying *ala* an elopement at Cinderella's castle. Maybe he was well and truly happy now. And if Liam could move on from losing his young wife, how come Tobias felt inescapably stuck in his own past?

"They took him to the ER," Liam said, clapping a hand on Tobias's shoulder to bring him back to the present. "That's all I know."

"Thank you. Thank you so much."

The two men exchanged nods, and then Tobias strode to the front desk to find out more. The receptionist paged a nurse's aide to take Tobias back to his grandfather and asked him to wait for just a few moments.

Every second that ticked by was torture. Somehow waiting here was worse because he was so close to finding out what he needed to know, to hugging his grandfather and telling him he loved him—just in case.

The doors behind him swung open, emitting a blast of balmy summer air and with it, a familiar face. A beautiful face with pale skin, dark eyes, and a hidden smile he longed to see.

Of course, Sally didn't seem to recognize him at first, but still he knew her instantly. She was every bit as beautiful as he remembered, and he was every bit as mortified upon recalling their last meeting.

He wished he could chase her down, ask her to dinner by making a self-deprecating joke about not force-feeding her this time—but these were wants, not needs. He *needed* to see his grandfather, end of story.

That was the only thing that mattered now.

He gave Sally a restrained wave and a smile of recognition. For a moment, they locked eyes. But then, just like that, she'd continued her journey down the corridor, and he could only watch her shoes pitter-patter across the linoleum floor as she hurried on to some destination he did not know.

"Mr. Lloyd?" a short woman in scrubs said, coming up beside him. "Ready to go back?"

Tobias tore his eyes away from Sally and followed the hospital worker back into the busy ER. St. Joseph's served a large cluster of small Texas towns, not just Sweet Grove, which meant it tended to be busy no matter what time you arrived.

The aide tried to make small talk about the weather and the local sports teams, but Tobias couldn't focus on anything besides finding his grandpa. At last she pulled a makeshift curtain aside to reveal Ernie Lloyd sitting up straight on the edge of the bed with his feet dangling off the side like a toddler.

Gramps tried to stand, but the aide shook her head and clicked her tongue. "You should be using this time to rest. Lay back. Let me cover you."

"I'm old, but I'm not an invalid," Ernie grumbled with a deep frown.

The aide nodded placatingly but still rushed to the old man's side to make sure he settled himself comfortably. Mechanical beeps, the squeal of poorly oiled wheels, and the various groans, coughs, and sighs of patients and their loved ones sounded all around them, forming the familiar symphony of the emergency room.

Tobias wondered if Gramps, too, was thinking about coming here with Grandma after she had suffered her heart attack. She'd taken her last breath here… or on the way here, at least, not even making it to the hospital but rather dying on the ambulance ride over. Tobias knew that no matter how much time passed, his grandfather still missed her every single day. He'd always wondered, too, if a part of his gramps might not mind kicking the bucket so that he could go on to be with his beloved wife once again.

"*Kleiner*," his grandfather said after he and the aide had reached some type of compromise on the best position for him to take within the bed. "It's good to see you, but what are you doing here?"

"Liam James called me. Remember?"

The aide motioned to a plastic chair in the corner on her way out, but Tobias declined the opportunity to sit. He'd had a hard enough time staying seated on the two hour drive over. Now he needed to stand, to pace, to let his grandfather see just how much he'd worried his only grandson.

"Oh, yes. That feels like weeks ago. They've been keeping me back here so long, but *really,* I feel fine. You didn't need to come all this way."

"Have they told you what's wrong yet?" Tobias paced along the edge of the room with the curtain, back and forth, back and forth in the tiny space.

"Low blood pressure. They're running some tests to find out why. Will you just stand still for a moment?"

Tobias nodded and forced himself to sit. "Well, that's not so bad."

"As I said, it's not such a big deal. Now tell me about your job interviews. Has anyone snapped you up yet?"

Tobias sighed. "Not yet, and I've been on dozens of them."

Gramps swore loudly in his native language, and Tobias hoped there were no other German speakers within earshot. "They're idiots. All of them."

"I'm glad you've got my back, Gramps, but that doesn't exactly help get me the job. Does it?"

The old man grumbled and pushed his feet back over the edge of the bed, then pulled himself into a sitting position. "Maybe you don't need them. I'd always thought you'd gotten the entrepreneurial gene from me. How about going into business for yourself?"

"That's a nice idea, but I don't know the first thing about starting my own firm. And I don't have the money to do it, either. I already owe over one-hundred thousand for my student loans."

"Would you be willing to try if I helped?" Gramps folded his hands in his lap and waited.

Tobias frowned. His grandpa was a proud man, and it had never been easy to say no to him. Still, he had to try to talk some sense into the old guy. "You've already got enough going on with the restaurant, and now your health, too."

"I told you this health thing is nothing, and the restaurant is fine. What I want more than anything is for you to be happy, *kleiner*, and I don't think you will be working for somebody else. At least not for long. It's time you stopped blowing in the breeze and put down some roots. Wouldn't you agree?"

FIVE

Yes, Sally did recognize Tobias the moment she saw him storming through the halls of St. Joseph's. What she couldn't recognize was the hungry expression in his eyes. No one had ever looked at her that way before, and she wasn't sure whether to feel flattered or outraged.

But as luck would have it, she didn't have time to stop and figure things out—not when she was already late for support group. She herself now hurried through the hospital corridor and let herself into the small meeting room as quietly as she could manage. Still, every set of eyes turned toward her as they all fell silent, waiting for her to take her seat at one of the back tables.

The group leader, a psychiatric nurse named

Laura, turned toward her with an overextended smile. "Welcome, Sally. I was just going over the agenda for this month's meeting. Today we'll be focusing on setting healthy boundaries."

Sally nodded and reached into her purse for a notebook and a pen.

Slowly, everyone shifted their focus back toward Laura, freeing Sally from the heat of their collective gaze. Perhaps she was a little bit like her aunt after all. That was one of the first things they taught in group —that many of the mental illnesses suffered by their loved ones are genetic. Also that they *are* illnesses, just like diabetes or cancer.

Sally was the only caregiver to an agoraphobic relative here, but there were many who lived with loved ones who had disorders on the anxiety and depression spectrum. Some of the people even had schizophrenics in their lives, which served as a stark reminder that things could always be much worse.

The support group had been Aunt Fiona's idea. She'd had this lightbulb moment after becoming involved in an associated online chat loop for people with mental health issues that largely impacted their day-to-day lives. Sally could still remember the sheen of her aunt's eyes as she apologized for holding Sally back and begged her to attend the support group to help minimize any damage to her life outside of Fiona.

But the truth remained Sally didn't actually have a life outside of her aunt's. Sure, she left the house to go to work each day, but nothing else really ever stuck. Maybe she was depressed herself, or maybe she'd just been born and anchored to the wrong town.

She often thought of what it would be like to live in London, Paris, or New York City—the kind of place where it was easy to blend into the crowd, where the very life and culture of the city carried you along like a rising tide. Yes, Sally could have been a different person if she'd been born to a different place, one that suited her better.

But here she was in Sweet Grove for her entire life, or at least for the rest of Aunt Fiona's.

She hated thinking that she would one day lose the one person who loved and understood her. Because, for all her faults, Aunt Fiona knew Sally inside out and always tried to do what was best for her beloved niece. It wasn't Fiona's fault that she couldn't leave the house without suffering a massive panic attack. And maybe it wasn't Sally's fault that no one in Sweet Grove much cared for her.

Yes, she'd been born in the wrong place.

One day she would leave it all behind and become who she was really meant to be. Until then, she would be Aunt Fiona's eyes and ears to the larger world outside. She'd attend group once per month, work her job at the library, and dodge any of the mayor's attempts to make her do more. In whatever spare time she found, she'd work on her novel.

Only she really needed to start over with a fresh hook, one that didn't involve the cruel fantasy that one day Ben could be hers. Ben was the past—an imagined past, at that—and she needed to look forward into the future.

Okay, fine. But why was there no light to illuminate the way?

Tobias pulled himself to his feet the moment the doctor pushed back the curtain and stepped into the makeshift room. He smiled and extended his hand, hoping that good manners would somehow help bring about the news he wanted to hear—that everything was fine and Gramps would live to a ripe old age. Maybe even set a record for Sweet Grove, for Texas, for the whole country.

Because Tobias doubted there would ever be a day that he didn't need his grandpa at his side.

"Looks like we have a bit of good news here," the

52

doctor said, clicking his pen in one hand while reading from the clipboard clutched in his other.

Tobias let out a long, happy sigh he hadn't realized he'd been holding back until the inhale that followed made him feel as if he could float.

"You're dehydrated," the doctor continued, glancing up at Gramps. "That's an easy fix. Drink more fluids, eat more regular meals, and your blood pressure should behave. Which means no more fainting spells."

Tobias smiled with relief and looked toward his grandfather who appeared to be anything but happy.

"*Great,*" the old man grumbled. "So I lost a whole day's work and whatever this trip cost to find out that I need to drink more water?" He stopped and chuckled to himself. "I already knew that."

The doctor quirked an eyebrow. "Did you? Because it seems your body had to take pretty drastic actions to remind you. At your age, you really can't risk—"

"Yes, yes, I know. I could fall and hit my head or break a hip. *Ahh,* the perils of being old." Gramps stretched like a lazy cat in the sun, pleased with himself for reasons Tobias couldn't quite understand.

"Thank you, doctor. I'll make sure he behaves," Tobias said with a warning glance toward his grandfather before reaching out to shake the doctor's outstretched hand.

The doc lowered his voice conspiratorially, leaning in close to whisper, "Get him on a regular schedule. That's the best you can do with difficult ones like him." Returning his voice to full volume, he smiled toward Gramps and said, "I'll send a nurse back to finish up, and then you're free to go."

"I may be old, but I'm still capable of taking care of myself!" Gramps called after the doctor as he shook his head and headed off to see another patient.

Tobias sighed. "Why do you have to make everything so hard? You know he's just trying to help."

"I don't need some young buck telling me to drink more water. I was already running a successful restaurant back when he was still in diapers."

"Gramps..." Tobias pinched the bridge of his nose to stave off the rapidly building headache. "Is there something you're not telling me?"

"Everything is fine and dandy, *kleiner*. Don't worry about me." The aged man struggled to slide off the bed and regain his footing.

Tobias rushed to his side and offered his arm for support, but Gramps refused to take it. "But if I don't, who will? Honestly, Gramps, you spend all day working in a restaurant. It's not like food and water are in short supply."

His grandfather shrugged but kept his intense gaze on Tobias. "You were at a job interview when it happened. Do you think that means something?"

Not this again. Tobias had already decided to return to Sweet Grove and open his own firm, but he didn't want Gramps to know it was because of his bad behavior. The last thing the stubborn old man needed was justification for failing to take care of himself. He leveled his grandfather with a judgmental expression. "When what happened exactly? When you decided to stop eating and drinking or when you passed out?"

"You know what I mean. Do you think it's a sign?"

"A sign you need to take better care of yourself? Absolutely."

Gramps's eyes sparkled with mischief as he revealed what he'd been thinking all along, "A sign it's time for you to come home to Sweet Grove."

"Not this again." Tobias glanced around for the nurse, but she was nowhere to be found. How long would they leave him and Gramps waiting in close quarters like this? Because Tobias didn't think he could resist the other's arguments for much longer. If they had to wait too long, Tobias may even find himself winding up on a blind date with some nice girl from the old country—and that was absolutely the last thing he needed at a time like this.

"Don't make me say it." The old man's smile was so broad, Tobias half expected it stretched around to the back of his head.

"What? That you need me?" Tobias could be stubborn, too. He'd learned from the best, after all. If Gramps wanted to tell him something, then he needed to say it with words.

The old man sighed in exasperation. "Yes, I need you. Of course I need you! But you need me, too. That's why none of the interviews have panned out yet, that's why I ended up here, that's why you're back."

"So you want me to do my job search from here in Sweet Grove and look after you and the restaurant while I do?" If this was how things were going to be, then why did he even go to law school? He'd been helping to run the restaurant for years. And while he knew it was Gramps's dream come true, it had never been his.

"No, you leave the restaurant to me," his grandfather said, making the entire conversation far easier on Tobias. "If you start looking after it, you'll never stop. Besides, it gives me purpose, which is important when you're my age. It's important at your age, too."

Tobias blinked hard. A purpose was the only thing he'd ever really wanted for himself—to show his mother that he had been born for a reason, that God had a plan for him, even if she didn't.

"So I come home and…" He let his words trail off, waiting for Gramps to finish them for him.

"Live with me. Consider opening up your own practice. Either way, you'll have time to know for sure where your next step should lead you."

Tobias nodded at last. He never could say no to his grandfather.

SIX

Another three weeks passed slowly by. Sally had reached both a dead end with her writing and an impasse with Mayor Bryant, unfortunately. When she'd started delaying responses to his emails, he'd begun to call her at her desk to plead his case. If she didn't give in soon, he'd likely commence in-person visits, and as the truest kind of introvert, that was the last thing Sally wanted—or needed.

"It's only a little thing to add to your schedule, but it would be a big help for me. Besides, the festival is still months away. You have time," the mayor argued now in the exasperated voice he seemed to reserve exclusively for Sally.

"Planning the fall festival is not a little thing," she grumbled into the receiver, contemplating cutting the cord on her desk phone so she could claim technical

58

difficulties. "And it has nothing to do with books! My job is to look after the library, not manage the town's social calendar."

"Sally, look. I wouldn't be asking you if I had other options. You think I like hearing how little enthusiasm you have about this? Because I don't. At the end of the day, you're a government employee, and our local government is run by me and by the chamber of commerce, who also thinks you're the perfect person for the job."

Sally snorted. "So that's it, then. I've been voluntold."

"Welcome to the planning committee," the mayor said with an obvious smile in his voice now that he'd won. Sally briefly thought about tendering her resignation and running away to some remote island where she could be alone with books, but her boss was one step ahead of her. "We meet the third Tuesday of every month at seven. See you next week," he concluded before ending the call on these closing words.

Sally jammed the phone back onto its cradle. She didn't even like attending Sweet Grove's Fall Festival, and now she'd be running it? What a cruel joke to put her in charge of organizing a good time for people who she didn't even really like all that much.

By trying to bring her into the town's social

circle, Mayor Bryant was pushing her ever further outside of it. If only she could pack up and leave right now. She didn't even need an island paradise filled with books. Maybe she'd just head to Scarlett's place in Anchorage, ask her to put her up until she found a job.

If only, if only…

"You don't look too happy to see me." A familiar voice floated from above her, and it was only then she realized that a patron had wandered over to her desk with a stack of books ready to be checked out.

It was a patron she hadn't expected to see around town now that the summer was nearly over.

"Tobias?" she asked, because that felt politer than asking what he was doing here. Wait… when had she ever worried about being polite? Why was she starting to now?

"That's me." He flashed a grin filled with uncertainty and something else she couldn't quite put her finger on. "Nice to see you again, Sally."

She smiled softly, not opening her mouth to expose the gap between her two front teeth. Instead she scanned the stack of books he'd brought her, first with her eyes and then with her barcode device. "Local business laws, entrepreneur guides… Let me guess, you're starting your own law firm?"

Tobias's eyes widened, and he regarded Sally as if

she possessed super powers. "I do want to open my own practice. How'd you know?"

They both laughed. It felt good. Real good.

"I'm kind of an expert when it comes to reading between the lines," Sally quipped, gesturing toward the stack of books with her shoulder. "Does this mean you're back in Sweet Grove to stay?" She hated how much hope had crept into her voice, how much his answer seemed to matter to her future happiness. She still didn't know why she liked Tobias as much as she did. He wasn't as handsome as Ben, nor was he as friendly as some of the other men about town like Jeffrey Berkley and Tucker Bennett. He wasn't rich like Liam James, or confident like the Bryant brothers.

So why him?

He studied her for a moment and wondered if, somehow, he had managed to read her thoughts. He *was* a lawyer. Did that mean he excelled at reading the words people only spoke to themselves? Did he already have her all figured out? And, if so, why did he still look at her like he wanted something more— something she had never offered to anyone but Ben?

Tobias rapped his fingers on her desk and gave her an awkward shrug. "I'm not sure yet. Just researching all my options before setting the course for the rest of my life. You know?"

She shook her head and looked away. She didn't know. Her life had already been pre-determined by a God who obviously hated her. First her parents had died, then her aunt had gotten stuck. The one man she dared to love would never love her back, and now... what could possibly happen next?

"You always knew you wanted to be a librarian, huh?" Tobias said, picking up her runaway train of thought and placing it firmly back on the rails. "I can see that. You probably made a card catalog for all your books when you were a little girl and then lent them out to your friends. Am I right?"

She laughed. It was like Tobias only saw the best parts of her, the parts she forgot to look at for herself. "You're half right. I did make a card catalog, but the only one who ever checked out books was my aunt. She always returned them just a little bit late, too, so that I could add her late fees to my piggy bank. I bought my first hardcover edition of *The Hobbit* that way."

Tobias chuckled as if he, too, could remember the whole affair as if it had happened yesterday. "She sounds like a riot. You should bring her into my grandpa's restaurant sometime. I'd love to meet her."

"We'll see," she answered simply, not wanting to ruin their banter by speaking the hard truths of Aunt Fiona's condition.

She scanned another book from his large stack, then paused. "You know, if you're really serious about opening up your own firm, there's a spot that recently opened up on Pine. It used to be a pizza place and before that a jeweler's and before that a thrift shop. People say it's cursed."

Tobias chewed at a fingernail as a way to hide his frown. "Fred's old place, you mean?"

She nodded.

He dropped his arms to his sides and cocked his head in thought. "That's actually not a bad idea."

"The curse doesn't scare you?"

"No, because I have a lucky charm."

"Don't tell me, you're wearing lucky underwear under those old jeans." She felt the heat rise to her cheeks and saw Tobias's turn brick red as well.

He winked at her despite their mutual mortification. "Nothing like that."

"Then?"

"It's you, Sally."

Suddenly her throat felt very dry. She coughed until she had tears in her eyes. Tobias stood before her a concerned blur. "Me?" she managed to squeak. "Why me?"

"Why not you?" he answered with another thousand-watt smile.

"I guess... I mean I... It's just that..."

"Stop, it's okay. I don't want to make you uncomfortable, but I do want to see you again. Will you come check out the place with me? Give me your thoughts? Help to counteract the evil curse and all that?"

"I…" She shrugged. What would she gain from saying no? And for that matter, what could she gain from saying yes? Her legs trembled beneath her and she pressed her hands down on her lap to help steady them. "Pick me up after work? At about five thirty?"

As she watched Tobias pick up his stack of books and walk back toward the exit, Sally's throat tightened and her heart clenched. What was she getting into? And, more importantly, once she was in, would there be any way out? Would she even want one?

By the time Tobias left the library, he had about three hours to kill before Sally's shift ended. He was supposed to be researching prospects, but the only thing on his mind now was how he could get her to grace him with a full-on smile, the kind that proudly showed off her most arresting feature.

He'd had crushes before. He'd had girlfriends before, too. But none had ever gotten under his skin the way Sally did.

Was it something about Sally herself, or was it simply a matter of timing?

Now that he'd finished his schooling, it was time to look ahead to what came next—to settle down, start a family. Could that be why he found himself mooning over Sally like some kind of lovesick puppy?

No, there was definitely something about the snarky, small-town librarian that he couldn't resist. And he'd only find out *what* by spending more time with her.

His heart sped up as he thought about the way their hands had brushed when she'd handed him his stack of books...

Oh, he had it bad.

Tobias opened up his web browser to search for local real estate listings just in case Fred's old place didn't turn out to be a perfect fit for his needs. He began to type, but then his fingers betrayed the original goal and instead spelled out: "Is love at first sight real?"

A seemingly never-ending stream of pseudo-science articles filled his feed, so he took a deep breath, buckled down, and got to reading. Tobias didn't like having his budding feelings for Sally explained away by surging endorphins or oxytocin spikes, though. Besides, how could that chemical stuff even be true? He'd seen Sally many times before.

They'd grown up in the same small town, for goodness sake!

Now that he thought about it, the wedding had likely been the first time they'd had a conversation. Love at first speak? Well, that at least was a possibility.

He'd always found Sally beautiful in the way that you acknowledged a pretty flower and moved on with your walk. His attraction to her, though, had never consumed him before, not like this. Not until he'd seen beneath the surface. That was where the real beauty of Sally existed.

Yes, he knew her reputation, knew she wasn't popular or even well liked, for that matter. Somehow that only made her more alluring to Tobias. She faced constant rejection but still didn't bow or break under the social pressure to conform. She was herself, for better or for worse. She was unapologetically here, and she refused to back away.

Tobias admired that strength. It was the kind he'd always sought for himself but never quite found within. Maybe by spending time with Sally he could absorb a fraction of that self-aware courage for himself.

For now, though, he closed out his Google search and mindlessly flicked over to Facebook in the adjacent tab. Would Sally be on his favorite time-suck of a social media site? And if yes, would she accept a friend request from him… or was it too soon? Was he coming on too strong, or not strong enough?

Oh, he would drive himself crazy if he wasn't careful. No wonder they called it "falling" in love. Every time he tried to hold himself back, he found his thoughts tumbling forward—toward her.

A quick search for "Sally Scott" on Facebook didn't return a profile for her. He guessed that made sense if she didn't have any friends she wanted to stay connected with. They'd have to keep in touch the old-fashioned way—through phone calls and in-person visits—that would be a much better way of getting to know each other anyway.

He did find a profile for a Fiona Scott in Sweet Grove, but her page was listed as private and they had no mutual connections. Could this be a relative of Sally's, or just a mere coincidence?

He sent her a friend request, just in case, and then began to mindlessly scroll through his newsfeed.

Jennifer and Liam were celebrating their six-month anniversary, which she jokingly called their "half-aversary." She posted an entire album of photos showing her, Liam, and his little girl—now *their* little girl—over the last several months. They were a family now. No one would ever have guessed that their lives had been touched by tragedy or loss, not with the huge smiles they each wore as they beamed into the camera.

Ben and Summer Davis were thinking about getting a puppy and wanted to know which breed was best. Even Gramps was on Facebook these days, sharing some article that Tobias sincerely hoped was fake news.

He moved through his feed, smiling, wondering what Sally would post were she there, too. Would she talk of their meeting today? Would she post something noncommittal about being excited for that night then refuse to answer when people asked why?

Another post caught his eye, yanking Sally from his mind within a fraction of a second: *Anna Lloyd married Joe Wagner today in San Francisco.*

Several dozen people had already liked and commented, but he didn't recognize a single name among the well wishers.

Did he really mean so little to his mother that she hadn't even thought to tell him she'd be getting married? Did Gramps know?

He slammed his laptop shut, not wanting to think about his mother a second longer than he already had. He tried to focus on his plans with Sally for that night, but every time he tried to get lost in that daydream, his mother's face popped into his head.

He hadn't been good enough for her.

How could he possibly think he'd be good enough for Sally?

SEVEN

The library fell quiet for the rest of the afternoon, giving Sally time alone with her manuscript. Rather than writing forward, she decided to go back and revisit her earliest pages. And as she read over the words she'd once penned with so much passion, her stomach roiled with embarrassment.

What was I thinking?

The story that greeted her was a fantasy romance where Summer was the villain and Sally rode away into the sunset with her hero Benneth. She cringed as she remembered the glee that had pulsed through her veins as she rewrote her life story. She'd pictured herself as the Princess Bride and Ben as her Westley.

What. A. Joke.

The biggest joke of all, of course, was Sally herself. She'd been writing escapist fan fiction based on her own life. She'd spent years pouring over all the literary greats—Austen, Dickens, Tolstoy—and yet when it was her turn to take pen to page, this is what she produced?

She held down the backspace on her keyboard and watched as one by one the egregious sentences disappeared. Gone was the scene were Benneth and Salin shared their first kiss. Vanished was the part where Salin first laid eyes on her hero across the annals. It all disappeared with a few well-placed strokes on her keyboard.

Did this mean she would finally be free of the hold Ben had on her heart?

She couldn't say for sure, but she did know she was free to start again with her novel. To write something different, healthier, better.

The cursor blinked over the white page, inviting, begging Sally to add the first words of her new story. She took a deep breath and began:

There once lived a girl with impossibly light skin, a willowy build, and courage that roared through her veins like a mighty river. She grew up believing in fairytales, but now looked back on these childish dreams with consternation. She had no castle, no prince, but she did have

*more than her fair share of dragons to conquer.
And conquer them she would, otherwise what
kind of story would this be?*

Sally chuckled to herself as she continued clacking away at the keys. She didn't look up from the screen again until she felt a presence looming near her desk.

"Is it 5:30 already?" she asked with a satisfied smile as she turned to greet Tobias.

"Well, I'm a few minutes early." He motioned toward the screen. "Please, you don't have to stop on my account."

She glanced toward the word count at the bottom of her screen and was stunned to see she'd written several thousand words in the span of a single afternoon.

Wow, that certainly hadn't happened before.

"I was just finishing up, actually." Sally made sure to save her manuscript to the cloud before shutting down her computer for the day. "Ready to go?"

"You betcha." Tobias motioned for her to walk ahead, and she wondered if he would use that opportunity to take in her view from behind. The thought made her flush, especially since she hoped he would.

She liked that Tobias found her... compelling, if nothing else. She liked the way he focused on her as if she were the only thing worth looking at, listened to her as if what she had to say was important.

She hadn't said much to him, nor had he to her, but maybe tonight would be the night all that changed. Suddenly, she wanted to tell Tobias everything—about Ben, her aunt, even her novel. But no, that would only scare him away.

He'd run, and fast, if he knew how much crazy lay hidden inside. He'd look at her the same way everyone else did—as if she were the embodiment of an unpleasant odor or an inconvenient roadblock. She couldn't stand the thought of him turning his nose up at her the way everybody else in her life had always done.

For whatever reason, she wanted him to stick around for a while—and he wouldn't if he met the true Sally, the one that had never been good enough for anyone in her life.

"You look lost in thought," Tobias said as he held the door to his old, but pristinely kept, car open for her.

She put on her best smile, making sure to keep her lips closed to hide the imperfection that lay plainly between her two front teeth. "Not lost. Just excited," she admitted as she reached for the seatbelt buckle and settled in for their short ride.

"Is that so?" Tobias traced his way around the car,

then sunk down into the driver's seat. He turned to glance at her for a moment before sticking his key in the ignition and bringing the engine to life. Being with him was bringing parts of Sally back to life, too. And this time, she couldn't mess it up.

She'd been too honest, too vulnerable, with Ben. For Tobias, she needed to be strong.

It was the only way he might one day love her.

And if he loved her, maybe she could find a way to love herself, too.

Tobias watched Sally from the corner of his eye as he pulled onto Main Street. Her cheeks glowed pink and she wore a small smile as she watched the town of Sweet Grove glide past her window.

"What are you so happy about today?" he asked, unable to resist his curiosity.

Sally turned toward him, the smile wiped clean from her face. Her eyes wide and suddenly empty. "Oh, nothing," she answered dismissively.

He frowned. Why was she so intent on keeping him at an arm's length? The moments she let little bits of herself shine through were the ones that convinced Tobias she could be the girl for him. He had to find a way through to her, a way to keep her smile around. And he would. "Obviously it's not *nothing*. Tell me."

Her coy grin returned for a brief moment before she once again fought it off. Her voice came out measured and slow, as if the emotion was being restrained in her speech as well. "I made good progress with my book today. That's all."

So she liked to read. That made sense, given she'd become a librarian. But what was so private about a book? Why was she so loath to discuss it? He tried to keep his enthusiasm in check, hoping it would help her open up a bit more easily. "Oh, what are you reading?" he asked as he slowed for a stop sign. "Anything I might like?"

Sally turned her eyes toward her lap and murmured. "Not the one I'm reading. The one I'm writing." She spoke so quietly he almost missed it. It took him a moment to realize what she'd just confessed.

"You're writing a book?" he blurted out, full of zeal despite his earlier attempts to restrain himself. "Sally, that's awesome. And so impressive. Wow."

That same fleeting smile lit up her features again. This time it blinked on and off as if the expression couldn't be sure whether it wanted to stay or not. "It's no big deal," she murmured.

"No big deal? It's huge, actually." He waited at the

stop sign, thankful no other cars had lined up behind them. "Everyone says they want to write a book, but few actually do. Heck, *I* want to write a book."

Her eyes locked on his, a newfound confidence glistening within them. "What would your book be about?"

He shrugged. The goal was to talk about Sally, to get to know her, not share more of his own mediocre accomplishments. He moved the car back into drive as he spoke. "Sometimes I write my thoughts down as a way of getting through the day. Mostly journal entries. Some poems. Occasionally a short story."

"So you keep a diary?"

"Yeah, I guess I do." He turned toward her to gauge her expression and liked what he found waiting there.

Sally studied him for a moment longer, before finally letting a full smile settle on her face. "Does it help? The diary, I mean?"

"It does when I actually get the courage to write in it."

"What do you mean?"

"Sometimes I'm afraid," he admitted, hoping she wouldn't perceive him weak after this confession. He suddenly understood Sally's hesitation in sharing about her writing. Those words on paper were so deeply personal. If someone didn't like them, did that mean they didn't like you? Didn't like the core of who you were?

"Afraid of having to acknowledge what you're feeling?" Sally asked gently.

He turned toward her, swerving slightly as his eyes left the road. "You... you understand?"

She nodded, then looked away, bringing a hand to rest on her chest as she spoke. "It's like putting your feelings into writing makes them more real, gives them power you may not be sure you want those words to have."

"I wouldn't have said it that way, but yeah. You're exactly right. Is that what working on your novel is like?" Words had staying power. They gave a voice, a legacy—and that was exactly what Tobias needed in order to prove himself. Maybe one day he'd progress beyond his diary and short stories, but at the same time, he liked the idea of writing much more than the act itself. The way Sally spoke about her craft suggested her feelings were entirely different. Opposite, even.

"In a way. I'm afraid I'm not a very good writer." She frowned for a moment, but then the smile returned. Voicing her insecurities aloud seemed to help her in some odd way.

"Don't be modest. I'm sure it's wonderful. Would you consider letting me read it one day?"

Horror flashed across her face. She cleared her throat before speaking what seemed to be very carefully chosen words. "Maybe. Maybe one day. Modesty has never been a problem for me. Believe me. If anything, I have the opposite problem."

"So you're conceited?" He laughed at the ridiculousness of this suggestion.

But Sally didn't join him. "Clearly something is wrong with me. Nobody in this town likes me, except maybe for you."

He reached for her hand before he could stop himself. "*Definitely* me."

"But why?" she asked hardly above a whisper as her hand shook within his grasp.

"Why not?"

"That's not very reassuring," she said with a sigh.

"I just feel we understand each other. Don't you?"

"So what you're telling me is you're damaged, too." It wasn't a question, but rather a conclusion. Moreover, it was the right one.

"Yes, I am," he said without hesitation. *So much more than you know.*

She gave his hand a squeeze. Maybe to say *thank you*, or maybe to say *welcome to the club*. Either was fine by Tobias.

"How so?" she asked.

Tobias pictured himself sharing his life's story

with Sally, letting her know all about the mother who hadn't wanted him, the father who had never met him. He wanted to confide in her, but he just couldn't. Not yet.

"That's a topic for another day, I think," he said so quickly the words jumbled together. "Hey, before we hit Fred's old place, let's stop in at my gramps's restaurant and grab some food. You must be hungry, right? Now that we have a smile on your face, let's get some meat on your bones."

Sally let go of his hand and returned her gaze to the outside world. Just as she'd begun to open up to him, he'd forcibly shut her out. Sometimes he could be so stupid. Especially, it seemed, when it came to Sally Scott.

He said a quick prayer in his head asking for strength, begging that he hadn't ruined his chance with her when she was the single thing in the world he felt most excited about these days.

If only he knew whether she felt the same way...

EIGHT

Sally noticed how quickly Tobias changed the topic when she asked why he'd referred to himself as damaged. She couldn't fault him for wanting to hide—after all, she'd chosen not to discuss her family situation or her decades-long unrequited love affair.

Still, it was hard to imagine handsome, smiling Tobias could be harboring an ugly secret. He seemed so normal, especially when compared to Sally who never quite felt at home in her own skin.

Then there was the surefire fact that if she pushed him too hard about his hidden defects, he'd push back, wanting to know hers. And she wasn't ready to share, not yet.

She tried to smile but felt the expression fall from her face almost as soon as she'd made it once she realized that she'd smiled too big and shown off that hideous gap between her teeth.

"Why do you do that?" Tobias asked, turning into the parking lot at Ernie's German restaurant.

"Hmmm?" she asked through pursed lips.

"You smile, then you take it back. Almost like it was a mistake. Do you not like to smile?" He parked and turned toward her, expecting some kind of deeply personal answer, no doubt. She still didn't understand how he could read her so well when they'd become friendly only very recently.

"I was just thinking that yes, I'm hungry and I love your grandpa's food." She offered an exaggerated, toothless smile and pointed to her face for emphasis. "But then I thought..." She switched her expression to a cartoonish frown and pointed to her face with her other hand.

Tobias burst out laughing, and Sally forgot to maintain her scowl, joining him in the lighthearted moment. It was so easy to come undone around him, so dangerously simple.

"Then you thought...?" he prompted once they'd both sobered up.

"Then I thought," Sally continued with a scolding finger. "Do we really want a repeat of the last time you tried to feed me?"

Tobias hung his head in affected shame. His

happiness still came through loud and clear, however. "The infamous meat event, you mean?"

She nodded as another tiny giggle escaped before she could swallow it back down.

"Of course, I want to revisit it. Only this time I'll act the way I should have the first time around."

"So a redo? You want a second chance?"

"I do."

"For what?"

"To be determined." His eyes lit with a flicker of mischief, then he turned away from her, opened his door, and climbed out of the car.

Sally quickly unbuckled her seatbelt and made her own exit.

Tobias shook his head. "Not going to give me the chance to be a gentleman, huh?"

"Not when I can open my own door just as easily as you can open it for me."

"Touché." Tobias's laughter floated over his shoulder as he walked past the main entrance to the restaurant.

Sally followed behind him, noting that Tobias was almost exactly a head taller than her. "Umm, I thought we were going inside?"

"We are. Just through the VIP access." He nudged open a heavy metal door at the side of the building and gestured for her to enter.

Sally stopped and studied him, a quizzical expression no doubt blooming on her face. Did he realize how much kindness shone within his sparkling green eyes, how safe his strong arms made her feel? Perhaps this was why she insisted on opening her own doors. Sally had never craved a hero before, at least not any other than herself. She'd loved Ben because of his vulnerability. With Tobias, everything felt different and new. And very, very exciting.

"At least let me open *this* door for you!" Tobias said with a drawn out sigh and goofy expression.

She giggled and went in ahead of him, then stopped as she took in the clean stainless steel counters and double stovetop before them. "It's smaller than I expected."

"Just Gramps back here most of the time. Now let's hurry before he turns up and asks us a million questions."

She thought about this for a moment, tilting her head to the side. "What kind of questions?"

"Do you really want to find out?" He opened the warming cabinet, releasing savory, starchy, buttery, and meaty scents into the room with them. "Mmm, perfect. I was hoping we'd find Knackwurst," he said, setting the pan onto the counter, then stalking back through the kitchen and grabbing a pair of styrofoam takeout containers to place the food into.

"Can I help?"

"Sure. There should be some fresh tablecloths over by the plates and glasses. Grab one for us to spread out."

"Spread out?"

"Yeah, we're going to the place where it all began."

Sally's heart dropped to her belly. "The wishing well?"

Tobias nodded, completely unaware of the reasons why she wanted to avoid the scene of Ben's wedding to Summer. Why, that was one memory she didn't want to revisit. Not ever.

"Umm, can't we just eat in here? There may be... bugs and stuff... Outside, I mean."

"Oh, Sally, don't you ever just give a guy a break?"

"Is it really that important to you?"

He nodded. "Let me get it right this time. Please. I don't like failing."

Although she wondered why he considered their original meeting a failure—especially considering the two of them were together on a maybe, kind of, pseudo date at that very moment—she nervously agreed. Maybe revisiting the place where her heart finally died and now lay buried would be easier in his company.

Maybe she could slowly begin to heal...

* * *

Together, Tobias and Sally trudged through the orchard to the site of the old wishing well. He, of course, insisted on carrying everything—still doing his best to prove to Sally that he was a gentleman, that it would be safe to open up to him, to let him in. He wasn't sure how well that plan was working out, though. The closer they got to the wishing well, the more she pulled back in their conversation.

"Okay, now what?" Sally asked with a sullen expression he just couldn't understand when they reached the scene of their first meeting. The field and hill around the wishing well seemed abandoned without all the wedding guests milling about. Now it was just him and Sally, and a few solid pounds of his grandpa's finest food to keep them company.

"Does this look like the spot to you?" he asked, wandering over to where he thought he remembered setting up for the wedding.

Sally shook her head. "More to the right."

He tapped his temple then gave her a quick thumbs up. "Ahh, yes. You have a really good memory."

She shrugged and wrapped her arms around herself even though it was at least eighty degrees outside. Sally continued to stand rooted to the spot even as Tobias laid out the blanket and unpacked the food.

"Are you ready?" he asked, glancing over everything one last time to make sure it was perfect.

She nodded, and Tobias watched as a tiny shiver ran up one arm and down the other. Taking his proffered hand, she gently arranged herself on the blanket and waited for him to guide her back through the recent past.

"Okay, so I started by yelling at you." He plopped down next to her with far less grace than he'd intended. He felt his face grow hot. They'd just begun this reenactment and already he was fubbing it up all over again. "That probably wasn't the best way to start, was it?"

A hesitant smile lit her face as she shook her head. "But there were a lot of people. I probably wouldn't have heard you otherwise."

"Good point," he said, then formed a funnel around his mouth with his hands. "Hey!" he whisper-shouted in her direction.

Sally laughed and moved closer to him on the blanket. Now their only a few inches separated her hips from his. "Do I look like I could use a good feeding?" she asked with a quirk of her lips.

"Actually," Tobias answered, keeping his eyes glued on hers as he spoke. "I just wanted to tell you that you're the most beautiful woman in this orchard, in the entire town of Sweet Grove, maybe even the world."

He watched with delight as a pink flush lit up Sally's features. "Oh, um… Thank you?" She scooted away again instinctively, leaving Tobias to wonder how he could get her to move in closer once more.

"Can I offer you some fine German cuisine?" he continued, gesturing to the food before them. Okay, so knackwurst wasn't exactly fine dining, but it was delicious—and perfect for a picnic like this one.

"As long as you don't try to force feed me," she said with a snicker.

Tobias rolled his eyes and puffed out his chest. "I would never do such a thing. Madame, I am a gentleman."

"Madame? Really?"

"Well, I didn't want to presume to know your name until you gave it to me. Hi, I'm Tobias Lloyd." He gave her what he hoped was his best, most charming smile.

"Hi. I'm Sally Scott," she said with a tiny wave.

"Sexy Sally," Tobias mumbled, enjoying the look of shock that overtook his companion's face.

"Now I'm sexy?" She laughed as if the thought of it were absurd.

"Actually, you've always been sexy, but more than

that, *you're beautiful.* And smart. And kind. And strong."

Sally shook her head and turned away. "And you're talking about me?" She tried to disguise her sadness with a laugh, but Tobias saw right through it.

"Who else would I be talking about?" he asked as he risked moving closer on his own.

Sally glanced toward the well and squinted as if she saw some kind of ghost visible only to her. "Why are you saying all these things?" she mumbled, casting her eyes toward the ground rather than turning back to him.

"Because they're true."

"Tobias… I'm not sure… well, I'm not sure what you're after, but there isn't anything special about me. People don't like me. I don't make friends. I don't belong, and I don't lead some exciting life that you or anyone else would want to be a part of."

He swallowed down a lump in his throat. It hurt him so much to hear her say these things about herself, especially since he could tell she believed them to be undeniably true.

"You are special," he argued. "I like you. I like you a lot. I want to be your friend. Hopefully maybe even more than that. So why does what anyone else thinks matter?"

Tobias thought about kissing her right then and

there, but he didn't want to frighten Sally off. She obviously still needed a lot of convincing and a healthy measure of time before he could ask her for anything more from their relationship. Right now, the simple joy of spending time with her would have to be enough.

"Are we going to eat?" she asked, shifting her gaze toward the containers of food, but still unwilling to meet Tobias's eyes.

"Yes, but first, I have a request."

She glanced up at him for a second. Something in his expression must have scared her because she looked away just as quickly.

He placed his hand on hers, hoping it would bring her back. He didn't continue until he had her eyes once again. The whole while he felt her pulse beat in time with his own heart—a synchronized dance between their bodies even though their heads were still getting in the way of what could be.

"You said you don't have an exciting life," he reminded her gently.

Sally nodded.

"Can you trust me to help change that for you?"

"Is that some kind of pickup line?" she asked with a nervous giggle, harkening back to their first meeting once again.

But he remained firm, serious. "No, it's *a promise.*

You deserve to have nice things, Sally, but more than things, you deserve to have nice experiences. A nice life. Let me help give that to you."

Her eyes widened, and she tried to look away, but Tobias squeezed her hand to bring her focus back to him. "How?" she whispered into the light breeze that surrounded them.

"I don't know yet, but I'm going to figure it out." Reluctantly, he let go of her hand and reached for the food they'd packed. He needed Sally to understand that his intentions were coming from a kind place and that the last thing he wanted to do was pressure her unduly.

It wasn't until he'd prepared both plates and handed one to her that Sally finally whispered, "Yes, okay."

He had her trust. Now it was time to figure out a way to earn it.

NINE

Sally arrived at work the next day feeling as if she'd just woken from a wonderful dream. Unfortunately, that all changed the moment she booted up and checked her email. No less than a dozen forwarded messages awaited her, all from Mayor Bryant regarding the Fall Festival that he now expected her to plan.

The worst one of all contained an outline of the meeting schedule and a list of volunteers that made up the planning committee. Right at the top of the list, of course, was Summer Davis, Ben's new wife and Sally's sworn enemy.

That's all it took for the stores of happiness she'd built up from her time with Tobias to evaporate into thin air. *Poof!*

Growing up, she'd often heard the expression

"comparison is the thief of joy," but she'd never truly understood it until Summer Smith—now Davis— had usurped her entire life. Sally's heart quickened now as it pushed blood through her veins. It was one thing to have her would-be life stolen out from under her, but quite another to constantly be reminded of it.

Why couldn't the mayor just let her be? Why didn't Summer know enough to leave her alone? But, most of all, why did Sally think she had any business trying to find happiness with someone new?

If she let herself care for Tobias too much, the world would take him away, too. Just as it had done with Ben at his wedding and with her parents in their car crash so many years ago.

Once, Sally had been a happy, normal girl. She had parents who loved her, friends, family, a home. Then one night that had all been taken away in an instant. Her Aunt Fiona had been visiting them. She'd already tucked little Sally in for the night when the police showed up at the door to make their grim announcement.

Sally knew something was very wrong when she heard the persistent rap at the door. No one ever visited after her bedtime, so who could be here now? She crept out of bed to listen, but only managed to catch snatches of the conversation at the front door.

"A terrible accident."

"Critical condition."

"Not going to make it."

Though Sally was young, she was also bright. These horrible words had been more than enough to make her understand.

She didn't see her parents again until the funeral. She'd asked Aunt Fiona how the car had killed her mom and dad that night when they'd ridden in it so many other times just fine. She'd also asked how come her mama's soft skin had turned into stone. Why her daddy wasn't smiling. Why he looked so serious.

Aunt Fiona just cried and hugged Sally tight, dribbling snot into her dark hair whenever she pulled her niece close.

A few months later, the two of them packed up and moved to Sweet Grove to start their bleak new lives together. Sally hated losing what little she had left, hated having to start over without the support of her mom and dad. What she really wanted was to go back in time, back to the town where her parents still laughed and played and read bedtime stories.

She didn't like this new place one bit, especially since all her classmates already had best friends, always leaving Sally as the odd one out. Some did try to reach out to her, though. They would ask her questions, but she'd refused to answer them. This whole venture in Sweet Grove was a temporary arrangement. She wouldn't be here long. That police officer would come to find her and tell her it had all been a ridiculous mistake, say that she could go back home now, that her parents were waiting. That they missed her.

But the cops never came calling, never said the words Sally longed to hear.

Instead, her new classmates started to say that Sally was stuck up, that she thought she was better than them. *Better than them?* Of course, that wasn't true. Sally just knew she didn't belong, that she could never belong.

It wasn't until the school year ended that she realized no one was coming to take her back home, that her parents were really and truly gone forever. By then, it was too late. The other children already hated her, said she was "not-nice Sally," and stopped inviting her to play.

Only two children were ever willing to give her a second chance. Only two ever showed her any kindness. They were the members of her gifted reading group, and they became her best friends. One was a little girl named Scarlett Cole. She also grew up to be a librarian and moved off to Anchorage.

The other was Ben Davis.

She trusted the first with all her secrets, and the second with all her love.

Until…

She shuddered as the memory of Ben's rejection crashed into her yet again. It burned even now. Even with the time she'd spent with Tobias, him calling her beautiful, wanting to make her happy.

Still, *still*, her heart ached.

Believing things could be any different had been a mistake.

She'd loved Ben her entire life, confided in him for years, and still he'd tossed her heart away like a wadded up piece of trash. Why would it be any different with Tobias whom she'd known for such a short while? There would be another Summer, another woman to take his love away just when it finally seemed within reach.

Of course there would be, because that was how things went in Sally's life.

It may not be exciting, but if she proceeded carefully, her life could at least be comfortable. It didn't have to consist of one hurt after another. Not if she stayed strong and stopped trying to convince herself things would ever be any different, that happiness was even attainable.

There were Summer Smiths in this world, and then there were Sally Scotts. She couldn't let herself forget which she was, which she'd always be.

It was time to draw the line in the sand, to back

away and never try to cross it again. Sally took a deep breath, grabbed her phone, and typed the only two words she needed to say in a quick but painful text to Tobias: *I can't.*

Tobias woke up feeling refreshed and full of optimism for his future. He thought only of Sally as he worked hard through the morning browsing local commercial property listings and narrowing down his list of possibilities.

Of course, they'd realized too late the night before that Sally and he were supposed to be viewing the rental at Fred's old pizza place rather than picnicking in the orchard. But every time he saw Sally, he seemed to lose his mind. And he wouldn't trade that time they'd had together for anything.

Now he wondered what great times may lay ahead. Would Sally be at his side for the grand opening of his future firm? Would they one day get married at the scene of their first real meeting, right there in the orchard with the whole town smiling up at them as they vowed to love each other forever in front of the old wishing well?

Anything was possible, and that was what excited him the most. Figuring out what would come next.

Proving to Sally that she wasn't as hated as she seemed to assume. Standing by each other as she followed her dream and he pursued his.

Always together. Happy. Loved.

What a life this could be!

After a long morning spent half researching for his firm and half daydreaming about Sally, Tobias popped into his grandfather's restaurant for lunch. That was when he received Sally's text. The words swum before his eyes, making him feel as if he needed to come up for air.

I can't.

"Can't what?" he typed back.

Be what you need me to be.

Tobias took a deep breath before texting his reply. He still couldn't explain how he had become so enamored of Sally, and he was still terrified of losing her, but it was too late to turn back now.

"It will hurt no matter what happens," he whispered to himself, "but maybe it can be really, really good, too. I know it can be." Besides, he'd already set the wheels in motion for a very special surprise he planned to present Sally with that weekend.

At last he typed his response: *I don't need you to be anyone other than yourself. But I do need you to come on a day trip with me this Saturday.*

"What's that, *kleiner?*" his grandfather said, joining him now in the kitchen.

"Just talking to myself is all," Tobias mumbled, watching his message change from sent to read, hoping the three little dots that meant Sally was typing would appear soon, that she'd agree, give him a chance to make her see how good they could be together.

"You know only crazy people talk to themselves, don't you?" Gramps said, reaching around Tobias for the garnish tray.

Tobias chuckled. "You talk to yourself all the time."

The old man smiled and tapped the side of his head knowingly. "Like I said, only crazy people."

"Well, at least I'm in good company, then." Tobias glanced back down at his phone. Still no dots from Sally.

"Who is she?" Gramps asked, leaning in close to peek at the phone in Tobias's hand.

He quickly pressed the button to lock his screen and hide his secrets from his grandfather's eyes—at least for a little bit longer. "Who said anything about a she?" he asked, shoving his phone back in his pocket.

"Your eyes. They told me everything."

Tobias scrunched his eyes tight in protest. He

hated how easily the old man could read him. This inexplicable awareness of Tobias's plans had foiled many of his youthful schemes. The last thing he needed now was for Gramps to make things harder than they already were with Sally. "You really are crazy. Do I need to take you back to the hospital to have your meds checked?"

"What's to be embarrassed about? So you're in love." Gramps chuckled as he finished plating his food and stuck it beneath the warmer. "It happens to the best of us."

"Love?" Tobias laughed off his grandfather's suggestion, even though he knew he was falling quickly toward that very thing. "No, I'm not even sure we've been on an actual date yet."

"So who needs to follow all the conventions when it comes to love?" His grandfather clapped a firm hand on his shoulder and smiled. "I knew I loved your Grandmama from the very second I laid eyes on her."

"Uh huh." Tobias appreciated his attempt at a pep talk, but had long known the actual truth behind his grandparent's courtship so long ago. Gramps claimed love at first sight, while Grandmama told a very different story of a cocky young man who barely gave her a second glance until almost a year had passed.

Gramps pressed down on his shoulder before

letting go and shuffling toward the other side of the kitchen. "What *uh huh?* It's true, and you know it. We had nearly fifty years together, we did. Good ones, too."

"And you knew it from the first second? The very first second?" Tobias used the opportunity to fish his phone out of his pocket and give it a quick check while Gramps's attention was focused elsewhere. Still no dots, though. It was as if Sally had turned her back on their conversation.

"Of course I did. It was like God whispered into my ear, 'there you go, Ernie. That one's for you.'" He returned to Tobias's side, giving his grandson his full attention once again.

"God?" Tobias wondered aloud. His grandfather had always been a man of strong faith, but he rarely discussed these private matters of the spirit with Tobias.

"Of course, God. Who else?"

Tobias stood mute, causing his grandfather to shake his head in consternation.

"Silly *kleiner*. How are you going to let a woman into your heart if you can't let God in?"

That was a reasonable question, but there was no real answer Tobias could offer in exchange. Recognizing their impasse, he decided to offer up another bit of information that he knew his grandfather wanted to hear. When it came right down to it, he would rather his grandfather meddle in his love life than his spiritual one. "If I tell you who she is, will you stop hassling me?"

His grandfather winked, which wasn't really an answer, but oh well.

Tobias took a deep breath and made his revelation quickly. "Sally Scott, the librarian. We ran into her at the wedding, remember?"

Gramps nodded and made a little grunting sound. "That is not who I would have picked for you, but then again, I'm not you."

Tobias bristled. "What? Why would you say that?"

"She's had a hard life, you know. Living with that aunt. I don't think she has many friends."

"What about an aunt?"

"Let her tell you. It's not my place."

"But…" Maybe this withheld bit of information would tell him what was making Sally so hesitant to let him in. He had to know, but he wished Sally would be the one to tell him.

Gramps changed the topic so fast, it took him by surprise. "Have you told her about your mother?" he asked abruptly. This was a great way to take him from moony to angry in a matter of seconds.

"Anna is *not* my mother."

"Well, it wasn't me who grew you in my belly, *kleiner*. Eventually you have to make your peace."

"So now I have to talk to Sally, God, and Anna. Anyone else?"

"You can always talk to me, too."

Tobias glanced down at his phone again. Finally a message from Sally had arrived.

Okay, it said. *I'll come.*

TEN

Sally tried to cancel on Tobias at least two more times before their outing on Saturday, but each time he convinced her to reconsider. It wasn't that she didn't look forward to time in his company. On the contrary, she looked forward to it *too much*—and that's what terrified her.

What would happen when the blinders fell off and Tobias saw Sally for who she really was? For someone unworthy? She didn't think she could take having her heart broken twice, and yet...

The smallest little part of her—a part so tiny she scarcely recognized it—believed that a happy ending was possible for anyone.

Yes, even for Sally.

So this left her at war with herself and with a difficult decision to make. She could avoid Tobias and possibly miss out on the greatest thing to ever happen to her, or she could take a chance, risk the hurt, and see where they might be able to go.

It all started—or perhaps continued—with whatever Tobias had planned for them today. Sally woke up early, unable to sleep when so many questions gnawed at her mind.

Tobias had promised a surprise outing. He also said he knew she would enjoy it, but he refused to reveal the secret plan ahead of time. What could it possibly be? Sweet Grove wasn't a large town by any means, and the nearest big city was at least an hour away. He gave no hints of any kind and wouldn't even tell her what kind of outfit she should wear.

Excitement and anxiety battled it out, overwhelming poor Sally who didn't know how to ease either. When at last Tobias arrived to pick her up for their big day, she'd settled on wearing her hair in a simple braid along with a loose, knee-length skirt, fitted T-shirt, and cardigan. Hopefully the outfit would work well enough in any setting to keep her from feeling out of place.

"Red," Tobias said when she opened the door and stepped out onto the porch. "I like it."

Sally gave him a closed lipped smile. The boldly colored lipstick had been an afterthought, but now she was happy she'd gone for it. "Thank you," she mumbled as she waited for him to trace his way back down the steps and lead the way to his car.

Instead of moving away, though, he surprised her by wrapping both arms around her waist and pulling her near for a hug. Their faces remained kissably close as he spoke. "Thank you for agreeing to come with me today. I was really worried you'd cancel again, but I'm so glad you didn't. And I can't wait for you to see what I have planned."

Sally gulped hard, fighting for her words. "Umm, sure thing. What are we... I mean, where are we going?"

"You'll see soon enough." He chuckled and gave her a tight squeeze before releasing her from the hug. His hand reached for hers as he led her toward the car and opened the passenger door.

"Hey!" Sally protested.

"Sally four, Tobias one. I'm catching up!" He pumped his fist in the air to celebrate this small victory.

She smiled to herself as she sank into her seat, loving how insistent Tobias was on treating her right. Even though his manners were a little old-fashioned, it felt great to have them focused on her.

"Where to, miss?" he asked, shifting the car into reverse.

Sally turned toward him as much as the seatbelt

tight against her lap and chest would allow. "You tell me!" she teased, still desperate to know their destination.

"Ha ha, nice try. You'll find out soon enough." Once Tobias had backed onto the street and shifted into drive, he handed Sally his phone.

She glanced down at the massive mobile phone in her hands. It was at least twice as big as Sally's even though they both had iPhones. "What's this for?" she asked, pressing the button twice to unlock the screen. "Do I need to call someone?"

"Nope." He held the end of the word extra-long, making a drawn-out popping sound with the *P*. "See if you can find the cable to hook it into the stereo."

She found the thin, white cable waiting for her in the glove compartment. When she plugged it in, the car's speakers immediately filled with a deep, gravelly voice. Not a song, but…

"An audiobook, oh! So this is going to be a long drive, I take it?"

Tobias gave her a satisfied smile before turning his attention back toward the road ahead. "I'll never tell. I figure you've probably already read this one before, but the audiobook is new and I thought maybe you'd like to hear it."

"Is this…?" Sally listened for a few moments until she recognized the flow of words and setting of the opening scene to the newest release from her very favorite author, the one she had told Tobias about during their second chance at a first meeting in the orchard.

"MC Raven's new one. Yup. I'm not usually a romance reader, but I think I'm starting to come around." He grabbed for Sally's hand again, and she let the warmth from his fingers spread all the way up to her heart.

She couldn't wait to see where they were headed.

Tobias glanced at the time on his car's dashboard. They'd be perfectly punctual for the day he had planned. Fortunately, he'd driven this same route many times before and knew exactly how to time the journey. He spotted the exit for his law school and merged into the right lane.

"Oh, are we close?" Sally asked as she rubbed her hands together in anticipation. The audiobook had kept her questions at bay for most of the long drive.

He nodded. "About fifteen more minutes."

As promised, they pulled into a long, winding driveway hidden within a giant cluster of trees no more than a quarter of an hour later.

Sally gasped when their destination came into

view. A tall chateau style house stood atop a hill surrounded by forest on either side. "Whoa! This place is enormous. Who lives here?"

"You'll see soon enough," he said, perhaps even more excited than Sally for the big reveal as he parked the car out front. Although Tobias had never been here himself, he, too, was impressed by the spectacle of the hidden mansion in the woods.

"Keeping your surprise to the bitter end?" Sally joked, stepping out of the car and stretching both arms overhead as she arched her back to rid herself of kinks that had formed during the drive.

"I like to think the end is actually quite sweet," he answered, focusing on Sally's lips as he spoke. "Go on. See for yourself."

"Together?" For the first time, Sally reached for his hand and not the other way around. And he eagerly accepted.

"I'm nervous," Sally admitted as they climbed several flights of stairs to reach the house on top of the high hill.

And he gave her hand what he hoped was a reassuring squeeze. "Don't be."

When at last they reached the door, Sally raised her fist to knock, but the door was flung open from the inside before she could complete the motion.

Across the threshold stood an eccentric old

woman with long, dark hair and holding a kitten in her arms. She wore a brightly patterned shawl draped around her shoulders and big, fuzzy slippers on her feet. Her voice came out deep and even. "Tobias and his lady friend," she drawled. "You're right on time."

"Thanks for agreeing to meet with us today," Tobias said, offering his hand for a shake.

When the old woman turned toward Sally, Sally turned white as a sheet. "I'm Sally. A-a-are you…?"

Ah-ha! So she *did* recognize her. Tobias had worried she might not since the reclusive celebrity rarely made public appearances these days.

"MC Raven in the flesh, at least for a little while longer." The old woman handed Tobias the kitten —"Here, hold this"—then wrapped Sally in a colorful hug.

"You-you're my favorite author," Sally sputtered, and Tobias could swear he saw the beginnings of tears forming in her eyes.

"So I hear," MC answered. "I also hear that you're an aspiring author yourself. Come on in, and let's talk shop."

Sally looked like she would either cry or faint or both. "Oh my gosh. Yes, yes, I would love to!"

The authoress chuckled and took the kitten back into her arms, then led them to a large, open living room and invited them both to sit on the Victorian style sofas that lined the corner of the room. "I'm going to go grab the snacks my helper prepared for us this morning. Make yourself comfortable and I'll be right back."

Sally's eyes darted all around the room, taking in the odd mishmash of classic English style and something straight out of Hobbiton. When at last she turned toward Tobias, her wide smile freely showcased the gap between her teeth that she normally tried to hide.

"It's magical," she said at last. "How on earth did you make this happen?"

"Well, you told me she was your favorite author, and I thought the name sounded familiar even though I'd never read her myself. I looked into it and turned out that my favorite professor also works at the firm that represents her estate. I called in a few favors—okay, really I begged and pleaded and told him that there was this very special girl I knew, and it would mean everything to her to meet her favorite author—and just like that, we had an invite to come out for the day for some private writing lessons."

Sally glanced up at him quickly before turning her gaze toward her hands, which she'd twisted together in her lap. "Tobias, no one has ever done anything this nice for me. From the bottom of my heart, thank you so much."

"That makes me sad to hear, because people should always do anything they can to make others happy, especially for someone amazing as you." Truth be told, Tobias had always been a kind-hearted person, but he'd never wanted to make someone smile as badly as he hoped to make Sally. With others, he'd always been trying to prove himself, to put himself in a positive light. With Sally, though, he only wanted to make her feel good.

And it seemed with this latest surprise, he'd done just that.

She blushed, the color of health returning to her cheeks for the first time since entering the house. "Stop saying that. I'm beginning to believe you."

"Good, then all is going according to plan."

"Tobias, really. I don't deserve any of this. I don't deserve you." She turned toward him on the sofa, unshed tears shimmering in her big eyes.

"Oh, Sally, you deserve so much more than I'll ever be able to give you." He brought one hand to her cheek, then the other. He hadn't planned to kiss her yet, but the moment felt so perfect, so right.

Slowly, he brought his face in toward hers.

She licked her lips in anticipation, and he could feel her heartbeat speed to keep time with his. And then…

"I hope you like cucumber sandwiches and macaroons!" MC Raven called out, returning to the living room with a plate bursting at the seams with a variety of English finger foods.

Tobias's hands dropped to his lap in disappointment at the same time, feeling wonderful that MC Raven was proving to be such a good host and awful that he had just narrowly missed his chance with Sally.

The moment gone before it even had a chance to play out.

"Let me help you with that!" Sally jumped to her feet and raced over to grab the tray. The look she gave him when she returned to the couch implied that their kiss would be completed when the time was right. That she wanted it every bit as much as he did. That this could—*it would*—work between them.

But first, they had to finish their writing lessons from one of the world's greatest living authors.

ELEVEN

Sally still couldn't believe that she was here in her favorite author's living room. She sat tall and focused against the hard couch cushions, not wanting to miss a single word—a single moment—of this amazing afternoon. Before she knew it, though, their time together was already winding down.

MC Raven shifted in her chair and adjusted the sleeping kitten in her lap. "Just keep going, Sally. You have everything you need to get started. All you need to do is believe in yourself and try your best. You'll end up rewriting most of the first book in edits anyway, but it's still the most important story you'll tell. The first is often the truest. It's the one that needs to be told."

The old woman rose slowly to her feet and offered

the kitten to Tobias again, who eagerly accepted the stirring ball of fur.

Sally jumped awkwardly to her feet, waiting for whatever parting words of wisdom her new mentor was willing to impart.

MC gave her a tired smile. "Go get out there and tell your story, and when it's ready, send it my way so I can forward it on to my agent. No guarantees, but you never know unless you ask, right? But first, come with me." The old woman put a hand on Sally's back and guided her into the kitchen.

Sally shot Tobias a glance over her shoulder, and he gave her a thumbs up with one hand while twirling a ribbon for the kitten with another.

"Thank you again for everything, Mrs. Raven," Sally said as they turned the corner into the enormous wood-paneled kitchen. "It's been a real honor."

The author waved her hand and motioned Sally closer. With a whisper, she said, "You know I'm not the most important person in this room, right? That boy, Tobias, he had to move heaven and hell to set up this meeting. I know because I'm not easy to reach. I keep it that way on purpose, but he was determined to do this for you, which is why I just had to say yes. I see it in the way he looks at you, you know. He loves you dearly, the kind of love that not everyone gets to experience in this lifetime. So grab it tight and hold on for the ride of your life."

Sally swallowed hard. "Thank you for saying so," she whispered back. "But Tobias doesn't love me. We've only recently become reacquainted, and we're just friends."

MC blew a raspberry, the suddenness of which caused Sally to giggle.

"Oh, please," the author continued. "He loves you, and you love him right back. The sooner you realize that, the sooner you can get on with your happily ever after. The pain you've had in your life will help to fuel your writing, but the love that boy has for you will feed your soul. And that's the best kind of love, anyway—the kind that comes on so fast and hard that nobody on this earth can stop it. It's why I write the kinds of books I do. Love at first sight is out there for the lucky few who know it when they see it. Believe me. It's waiting for you. In fact, it's right out there on my old couch."

Sally didn't know what to say to all that. She dearly hoped it was true, but what if MC had read the situation all wrong?

"Invite me to the wedding, okay?" MC said with a kindly wink and another pat on Sally's shoulder.

"Okay," Sally said at last. Not the most imaginative response, true, but she didn't really know what else she could say. Her favorite author had gone out of her way to be welcoming and supportive. And Sally had always admired MC for her talent and poise. She loved getting lost in the romantic fantasies penned by this old woman she knew had loved and lost so many years ago.

And now she claimed to recognize a great love story in Sally's own life. Could it be?

This excited her even more than knowing her completed book would be shared with MC Raven's literary agent. Sally wrote as a way of belonging to something bigger, and now it seemed she did. Tobias was a bit of a loner himself since he'd spent so much time away from town in pursuit of his studies.

Was her favorite author right about everything? Could these two outsiders allow each other into their hearts?

She returned from the kitchen and found Tobias with the tiny striped kitten cuddled to his cheek. She'd always been a cat lover, and seeing him show such love to the little animal made her heart melt for him that much more.

He waved its tiny paw in Sally's direction. "Hey, you… she's purring, come hear it!"

Sally closed the distance between them and sat beside Tobias on the couch, pressing her cheek to the side of the kitten's impossibly tiny face. Sure enough, the gentle rumbling of happiness filled her ear. "What a sweetie!"

"I'll take that," MC Raven said, sweeping over to them in a swirl of fabrics. "Going to need my therapy cat handy if I'm expected to make this crazy deadline. I swear, with each book they want it written longer and finished faster. Do you two need me to see you out?"

Tobias reluctantly handed the cat back. He and the little tiger kitten had become quite close during their writing lessons that afternoon, even though it only left MC's lap for short bursts to play with Tobias and Sally.

Sally hugged the author goodbye, then reached for her friend's hand. "I think we can manage," she said, knowing she was answering more than one question.

"Good. That's precisely what I wanted to hear," MC said, clutching the kitten to her chest with a far-off smile. "Remember to send me that manuscript—and that invite, too!"

"An invite to what?" Tobias asked once they'd shown themselves out and closed the heavy front door behind them.

Sally felt too overwhelmed to answer. Instead, she pressed her lips to his cheek in a chaste kiss. Their first.

"Don't worry about that," she said. "We've got all the time in the world."

Tobias opened the car door for Sally, delighted when she passed through without protest. "Not going to fight me this time, huh?" he asked with a bemused smile as he leaned against the car and gazed down at her.

She shook her head gently. "After you went through all the trouble to arrange today, I figured I might be able to compromise on this one thing."

He laughed, loving her so much in that moment the intensity of his affection took him by surprise. "Just this *one* thing?"

"We'll see."

They locked eyes for a moment, and Tobias wished they were at the right level to attempt their first kiss a second time. Unfortunately, trying to do so while she sat and he stood would likely end with him falling into her lap, which didn't seem like the best way to make this particular memory. He couldn't help but wonder if Sally was warring with this same thing as he jogged around the car and positioned himself in the driver's seat.

They had a long drive back to Sweet Grove, and

he found himself wishing he hadn't picked up the audiobook. He'd much rather talk with Sally after the special day they'd just shared. He'd honestly rather talk to her any day, but more than anything, he wanted her to enjoy the time they spent together.

"Want to listen to more of our story?" he asked reluctantly, trying to keep his face neutral as he backed out of the long driveway.

"Eventually," Sally answered with her eyes closed and her rested back against the seat. "But I'd rather talk if that's okay."

He grinned, so glad that they were on the same page. "That's always okay. What did you want to talk about?"

"Me." Sally opened her eyes and turned toward him by resting her cheek against the seat.

"Ahh, my favorite topic." He wanted to return her focused gaze, but the traffic wouldn't allow it, and he doubted she'd want him to pull over so early in their journey home.

Sally sighed, revealing exactly where this conversation was headed. "I can see that, but I don't understand."

"What's there to understand?"

"Why you like me so much. Why you'd go out of your way to arrange something so special for me when we hardly know each other."

They hardly knew each other, but already he knew enough. The very fact Sally questioned her worthiness is part of what made him like her so much. It's what made him feel that Sally could understand him better than anyone in the whole world, especially when at last he told her about his mother and the terrible start she'd given him in life.

He gripped the steering wheel tight. "It was no trouble to—"

Sally shook her head and interrupted with "MC told me that it was actually a lot of trouble on your part."

"Well, okay, fine. But I enjoyed doing it, especially once I saw how happy it made you." He'd have to tell her—and soon. He just hoped it wouldn't change her impression of him. They stopped at a red light, allowing him to turn toward Sally.

Her brow was pinched together with concern. "Why, though? Why do you care if I'm happy?" she insisted. "Why me?"

He sighed when the light turned green far too fast. He'd much rather have this conversation face to face, but Sally seemed to need it right now. Why couldn't she understand how special she was? And couldn't she see that he was even more damaged than she'd ever be?

"Look, Sally," he said gently as he pushed down

on the car's accelerator and switched lanes. "You can drive yourself crazy trying to understand the reasons behind everything that happens in life, or you can just let go and enjoy them. I know you're beautiful, smart, kind, and a million other great things I have yet to discover. I could spend years trying to figure out which of those things tipped the balance and made me fall for you, or I can forget the why and focus on *what* I'm feeling."

Sally sat in quiet contemplation for a moment before asking. "What are you feeling?"

"Isn't it obvious? I'm feeling like nobody has ever understood me the way you do. I feel like you're the most incredible person I've ever met, and I feel like maybe—perhaps definitely—you're the one I've been waiting for my whole life."

Sally lifted both hands to her mouth. To hide a smile? Shock? He couldn't tell. Not until Sally said, "Stop the car."

Still reeling from the boldness of his revelation and the suddenness of her response, Tobias pulled the car into a nearby McDonald's parking lot. Oh, he hoped he hadn't blown it. Of course he'd asked too much of her. He'd scared her away just like he'd done with his mother as a child. Just like he always did with the people who mattered. Why couldn't he learn?

He put the car in park and shifted in his seat to face Sally.

Surprisingly, the expression on her face wasn't anything like he'd expected. She didn't look angry, outraged, sad, pitiful... nothing like that.

In fact, he hardly had time to see her face at all before it was pressed against his in a sweet, life-affirming kiss. That was when his brain shut off and his heart took full control.

That was when he knew for sure. His whole life he'd been searching for a purpose, a way of proving that his birth hadn't been accident, that he was meant to be here...

And now, as their lips brushed softly against each other's, Tobias knew beyond a shadow of a doubt.

He was meant to love Sally Scott with everything he had.

And that was the greatest purpose he could possibly imagine.

TWELVE

S ally's pulse pounded so hard, it was the only thing she could hear as she pulled her lips away from Tobias's. Other than her ill-fated encounter with Ben, this was her first kiss ever.

And it was perfect.

Tobias cupped a hand around each of her cheeks and pulled her forehead forward to rest on his chin. "I'm falling for you so fast," he murmured into the softness of her hairline. "So very, very fast."

She didn't know what to say next, what she could say.

Sally had so little experience in this realm that everything with Tobias happened in new and uncharted territory. The only romance she'd ever been party to before now had been unrequited, and she'd been too focused on her studies in college—and too committed to her foolish crush on Ben—to think of her classmates as anything more than study partners, or occasionally friends.

But Tobias, he was so much more than that.

And each day she spent with him made her feelings stronger, but it also made her more afraid of getting lost in them.

Could love change her life? Could it change her?

It seemed silly to think that Aunt Fiona could magically be cured, that Sally could suddenly be liked and accepted by her neighbors. And yet...

Everything happening with Tobias felt like a miracle.

How else could she explain why such a handsome, intelligent, and thoughtful man would want boring, plain, uninspiring her?

"I like you, too," she offered at last, eliciting another sweet kiss from Tobias.

"But you still want to know why," he whispered, pulling back to search her eyes for an answer she didn't know how to give.

"Yes," she whispered. "It's hard to believe in something you can't understand."

Tobias rubbed circles on her cheeks with each of his thumbs as he spoke. "Maybe that's what you've been missing all along, Sally. Good things don't happen to you, because you don't believe they can."

She swallowed hard, unsure why her first kiss had turned into a philosophy lesson, a church sermon, or both.

"But I do," Tobias said with a sad smile. "And I want to tell you why."

"Tell me." She raised her shaking hands to cover his, wanting to kiss him again, to hear his explanation, to just be in his presence without saying anything at all. It felt so strangely fulfilling, so un-Sally that she almost wanted to cry.

He dropped his hands from her face and leaned back in his chair with a deep sigh. "I think I'm drawn to you because we're so much alike."

"How can that be when everyone likes you so much and they hate me?" Sally sat back, too, feeling cold and alone without his body right beside hers.

"They don't hate you."

She leveled her gaze at Tobias, causing him to squirm in his seat.

He shrugged before answering. "You wear exactly who you are on the outside. It intimidates them, maybe. Keeps them from getting close. But I hide my damage, so I don't have to see the look on everyone's faces once they learn the awful truth."

It took Sally a moment to realize the conversation had taken a very different turn. No longer about Sally, suddenly they were discussing Tobias and the damage he'd alluded to in the past. Could it really be *awful* as he said? Would it change how she felt about him? She hated this, hated that she might have love snatched away from her yet again.

"Wait." She grabbed his hand and held it tight to brace herself. "You've been lying to me?"

Tobias raked his free hand through his hair and let out a long breath. "Not lying, but hiding. And not just from you, but everyone. Only my gramps knows the whole truth."

"Which is?" She held her breath, waiting for the words that would take all the oxygen out of the car, all the love from her heart.

Tobias turned toward her with shining eyes, but an otherwise expressionless face. "I was never supposed to be born, Sally."

"What? How could you possibly say that?" This was not what she'd expected, not even close. How could this wonderful man even think this about himself? And why would he feel the need to keep it hidden?

Tobias let go of her hand and wiped it on his pants, stuttering as he spoke. "My mom got pregnant as a teen. She tried to abort me, but my grandparents stopped her."

It was true, then. Her great love almost wasn't.

She felt sad picturing a world without Tobias in it. "Thank God they stopped her," Sally murmured.

"Yes, thank God, because he's definitely the one who saved me. And more than once, I'm afraid."

Tobias understood her, because he understood suffering. He understood not being wanted, and what he'd endured was so much worse than anything Sally could even fathom. Suddenly, her problems felt very small and far away.

"My mom eventually left," he continued. "I only see her every few years, and it's always very weird to be around her knowing she hates me."

"She doesn't ha—"

"Yes, she really does. My own mother wishes I'd never been born. She blames me for ruining her life."

"I'm sure she doesn't…"

"I know, because she told me."

Sally felt tears prick at her eyes. Sally had lost her parents far too young, but she'd always had Aunt Fiona to advocate for her, to love her. How it must hurt Tobias to know his own mother wished he was dead. No wonder he hid the truth deep down inside. She felt wrong for making him share.

"We don't have to—"

"Yes, we do. I want you to know this about me because I want you to know everything. I want to share a life with you one day, Sally, and I can't do that

127

if I hold back. Especially the important things, the things that make me who I am."

"I understand, but I still don't get why you chose me," she confessed. "You've survived against the odds. You're still so young but already you've accomplished so much. And here I am, nothing special. I just—"

"No, don't ever say that about yourself. First of all, because it isn't true. And second, because that's the whole problem. You believe good things can't happen to you because you don't deserve them. I struggled with that quite a bit during my teen years, but at a certain point, I stopped fighting myself and started to *fight for* myself instead. I wanted to show everyone, myself, my mom, show God that I was born for a reason, that I wouldn't be a life wasted. I was going to do something extraordinary, to earn my spot in this world, whatever it takes."

"And so you went to law school," she finished for him, so very impressed with all he'd overcome.

He took another deep breath and reached for her hand again. "Yes. For a long time I thought that was the way. But then I met you, Sally, and now I'm not so sure."

She frowned. The last thing she wanted to do was to ruin all Tobias had worked for, to let him lose touch with the wonderful man he had become. "You don't want to be a lawyer anymore?" she asked. Her throat felt dry, each word an effort.

"I do want to be a lawyer, but I think I have something much more important I need to do with my life." Tobias's eyes shone again, this time with barely contained happiness as he shifted in his seat and pulled Sally close.

"What?" she whispered, feeling distant, as though this scene was happening to another girl, one who deserved a man as good as Tobias.

"Sally, I think God put me on this earth with one simple mission in mind. I'm here to love you, Sally Scott, and to support you. Can't you see? I once thought that to be important I needed to find a way to change the world, but now I know that it's not up to me. It's you, Sally. Those pages you shared with MC Raven today, they were amazing. You have a story to tell—an important one, too—and my job is to help you."

Sally's voice trembled as she asked one of many questions swirling in her mind. "How are you going to help me?" She still couldn't understand why Tobias found her so special. She'd never done a single thing to deserve this, to deserve him.

"By believing in you so hard that you'll have no choice but to believe in yourself," he said before placing another kiss on her cheek.

* * *

The next morning, Tobias attended the First Street Church Sunday service, hoping to bump into Liam James after the sermon. He loved the close-knit community here in Sweet Grove, having missed it dearly when away in the big city for his studies. Even though he felt he'd always kept others at an arm's length, home was still home and always would be.

Pastor Bernie, as per his usual, was in fighting form that day, pacing from one end of the pulpit to the other as he spoke passionately about fulfilling one's unique purpose. Somehow he always knew just what his congregation needed to hear. Today, it was Tobias's turn to wonder if the pastor was, in fact, preaching directly to him.

Tobias scoured the crowd for Sally, but she was sadly nowhere to be found. He hoped one day they'd be able to attend services together but knew he had to wait until she was ready to take this big step forward with him. Until then, he would make himself available to her as she struggled with her faith and finally found her way home. And as his grandfather had suggested time and time again, he would pray.

"Let us use our God-given talents to give the glory right back to God," the red-headed preacher said as he glanced around the sanctuary, locking eyes with several members of the church as he scanned the room.

When he looked to Tobias, Pastor Bernie continued. "After all, who gave you those brains, that passion for music, the ability to dance, to sing, to write, a lover's heart, a lawyer's tongue, a doctor's touch?" He smiled wide and pointed high above.

Bernie let the room fall silent as his words sunk in. This was a tactic he liked to employ as he was reaching the end of each sermon, and it was powerful. It had inspired Tobias to form his closing arguments for court in much the same way, though he hadn't gotten many opportunities to do so yet.

After more than a minute of measured silence, the pianist began to play a light, closing hymn.

"Let us rise," the pastor said before belting out the opening words to this week's final song of worship.

Tobias sang along loudly, too. For the first time in a long while, possibly forever, he knew he was exactly where he needed to be, that God had brought him home, brought him to Sally for a reason.

The moment Pastor Bernie gave his closing affirmation, Tobias bolted from the sanctuary and into the foyer so that he could intercept Liam before he headed to the parking lot. It didn't take long to spot him heading toward the Sunday school room to collect his wife and daughter.

Liam noticed Tobias and waved him over. "Great to see you here," he said, offering first his hand and then a hug. "Is your grandfather with you today?"

Tobias shook his head. "Not today. He hung back to get the restaurant ready. He usually goes to Wednesday evening service instead. Easier to find coverage for the restaurant then."

"Of course, of course." Liam nodded greetings to several other members of the congregation as they passed by before turning back to Tobias. "Well, it's good to see you today and to know your gramps is feeling well."

"Oh, yes. Definitely. Actually, I was hoping to run into you. Do you have a moment?"

"Sure. What's up?"

"I hear you help people evaluate and grow their businesses and—well—I was hoping you could help me with mine."

Liam's smile widened with genuine happiness for his neighbor. "You have a business? That's great. Of course I'd be eager to talk with you about it."

Tobias laughed nervously. "No, no. I don't have one yet, but I hope to open my own firm someday soon, and I'm having a hard time knowing where to start."

Liam clapped a hand on Tobias's back and pulled a business card from his suit jacket pocket. "I can help with that, too. Call me or shoot me an email and we can arrange to have lunch later this week. Maybe at your grandfather's place? I'll take any excuse to have some of his delicious cooking."

Tobias laughed again, this time finding himself at ease. "Sounds like a plan."

Liam's wife Jennifer and daughter Molly Sue joined them, each grabbing onto one of his hands and smiling.

Liam beamed brightly. His entire face came to life in the presence of his family. "I've got to see these two lovely ladies home now, but I'll see you soon!"

"Bye," Tobias called after them, watching how the three walked in perfect sync, made the perfect little family. Is this what the future held for him and Sally?

He said another small prayer, hoping with everything he had that the vision before him might reflect a tiny piece of what was yet to come.

THIRTEEN

Sally woke up earlier that Sunday than she normally did on a day off. So early, in fact, that she could have easily gone to church if she'd wanted to—and she almost did. *Almost.*

In the end, though, she decided she would need more time to explore this fledgling faith on her own. Her obstacles had always been personal, and until she could work to resolve them, she'd feel out of place among the congregants of First Street Church.

But because she was up early anyway, she decided to cook breakfast as a nice surprise for Aunt Fiona. Their black cat, Spooky, kept her company while she searched the fridge and cabinets for ingredients. Ultimately, they landed on bacon, eggs, crescent rolls, and freshly sliced cantaloupe with cottage cheese.

Her aunt appeared at the counter less than a

minute after the bacon hit the frying pan. She wore her hair in a high, messy bun and yawned so wide she could probably fit her whole fist in there.

"You're so predictable," Sally teased.

Aunt Fiona smacked her lips. "But you aren't, are you? Since when do you make us breakfast? Not that I'm complaining. Not one bit."

Sally shrugged. "It just seemed like a nice thing to do."

Her aunt pulled out a bar stool and plopped down. "Nope, you're not getting off that easy. Now dish."

Sally chuckled and plucked the first few pieces of bacon from the pan with her fork. "Do you want this bacon or not? Because I can cook it extra until it gets extra crispy and dried out."

Aunt Fiona looked scandalized. "You wouldn't dare!"

Sally handed the paper towel lined plate to her aunt and took another plate from the cabinet. "Don't worry. I know not to ruin perfectly good food."

"At least I've taught you something."

Sally checked on the rolls in the oven, then returned to the stove to tend the meat. "Actually, if you don't mind, I do have a question." She'd thought long and hard about whether to broach this topic with her aunt. With Ben not speaking to her, that only left her aunt with whom she could discuss Tobias, and—boy—did she want to discuss Tobias. It wasn't that she needed help, exactly. More that she just wanted to share, to know that someone out there was happy for her.

Aunt Fiona, of course, had no clue what was on her niece's mind. "You want money? Advice? A kidney? I knew you were buttering me up for a reason."

Sally laughed again. "No, none of that. I just want to know if you've ever been in love." For as much as the two shared with each other, they rarely talked about the past, leaving the time before her aunt had assumed guardianship of Sally a giant question mark in their relationship.

Fiona leaned back against her chair and made a low whistling sound. "Must've been at least twenty years ago, but yes. I was in love."

"What happened?"

Fiona blanched, and Sally almost felt sorry she'd raised this topic of conversation. Still, she needed to know. She had no one else to turn to, and she still needed someone to confide in about what was happening between her and Tobias.

"Aunt Fiona?" Sally pressed, her brown pinched now in worry. "Is everything okay?"

"Do you really want to know what happened?"

"Of course I do. That is if you're willing to tell me."

Her aunt pushed the plate of bacon aside and propped both of her elbows on the counter. "My sister and her husband died, and I became the sole guardian of an amazing little girl."

Sally's heart sunk. *"Oh."*

Her aunt chuckled, but Sally could tell she was forcing it for her benefit. "Chin up, buttercup. It was the best thing that ever happened to me."

"But you lost everything because of me." The timer on the oven beeped, but Sally ignored it.

Aunt Fiona was the one to rush over to rescue the finished crescent rolls. "No, that's not even the slightest bit true," she insisted, setting the hot tray onto a crocheted pot holder and coming over to offer her niece a hug.

Sally melted into her aunt's arms as guilt weighted down her limbs and caused her heart to sink. This was the same aunt who hadn't left the house in years, who needed to take anti-anxiety drugs just to speak to someone on the phone, and who'd apparently given up the love of life to be there for Sally when she'd been orphaned all those years ago.

"It's not your fault that I'm sick," Aunt Fiona said. "And it's not your fault that my boyfriend back then asked me to choose between you and him."

"He *what?*"

Her aunt nodded. "That's right. Al didn't want kids and told me I had to make a choice. Easiest decision of my entire life."

"Do you regret it?"

"Not even one fraction of one percent. Our love couldn't have been very real to begin with if he expected me to turn my back on my family in order to be with him."

"Then how do you know when love is real?" Sally whispered.

"Well, for starters, it's not the things we say. It's the things we do. That boyfriend of mine told me a million times he loved me, but the second I wanted to do something he didn't approve of, he was out of there." Aunt Fiona put a hand on each of Sally's shoulders and stared right into her eyes. *"That's not love."*

Sally smiled as she watched her aunt return to her stool and dig into her breakfast once more. "Yeah, I think you're right."

"Did something happen with Ben? Do you need to talk about it?"

Sally shook her head. It was strange discussing Ben with her aunt. Even though Fiona knew all about Sally's crush, they rarely discussed it. "No," she answered, taking more bacon from the stovetop and putting it onto a fresh plate for herself. "I know my love for Ben wasn't real."

"Okay, first of all, just because he didn't return those feelings didn't make yours any less real," her aunt said, waving a piece of bacon as she made her points. "Second, that boy is crazy not to snap you up while he had the chance. And third, *wasn't?* Does that mean Ben's in the past? Is there a new guy? And you haven't told me about him yet!"

"Hmm. So many questions." Sally laughed and popped a piece of bacon into her mouth, widening her eyes playfully at her aunt.

"Oh, you little brat!" Fiona teased. "You better tell your aunt everything, and you better do it right now!"

Sally grabbed the butter from the fridge, stacked the still very hot rolls onto a plate, and joined her aunt at the counter. "Let's see, I guess I should start from the beginning…"

* * *

Tobias and Liam met Tuesday for lunch, and by the end of that day, he'd hired himself a business advisor and was ready to take another very important step toward opening his own practice in

Sweet Grove. First, though, he needed his lucky charm.

He texted Sally to set it up. *What are you doing after work tonight?*

Her response came back to him immediately: *I don't know. What am I doing?*

Can I pick you up?

Okay. I'm off at 5:30.

I remember. See you then!

With their plan made, Tobias tried to return his attention to work, but he was far too excited to focus. Rather than wait around and procrastinate on his work, he decided to surprise Sally early at the library with a bouquet of flowers. The local flower shop, Morning Glory's, wasn't far, so he decided to park at the library and then walk over.

When he pushed the door open, a little bell jingled, and the town's resident gossip, Iris Smith, greeted him with a huge smile and open arms.

"Hey, stranger. I've never seen you in here before!" The florist gave him a tight squeeze before letting go. "This wouldn't be about the rumored crush you've been building on a certain local librarian, would it?"

"What? How did you know about that?" Of course, leave it to the Sweet Grove grapevine to always stay one step ahead. He tried to think of when and how this news could have circulated, but decided he just didn't care. The rumor was more than true, so the whole town might as well find out sooner than later.

Iris smiled mischievously. "I know everything that goes on in this town. And I'm right, aren't I?"

"Almost," he admitted, burying his hands in his pockets. "Except it's way more than just a crush."

The older woman clapped her hands together and squealed. *"Love!"*

Just then, the bell over the door jingled once more and a muggy summer breeze floated into the shop.

"Uh oh, Aunt Iris. I know that look! Who's in love?" Summer Davis ambled over with a giant computer bag at her hip. Her flip flops squelched with each step she took. Tobias didn't know Summer well since she'd only moved to town after he'd left for college, but he would forever be grateful to her since it was her wedding where he first really got to know Sally.

Iris gestured toward Tobias, and both women turned to him with dreamy expressions. "He was just about to tell us everything, too!" the older of the two exclaimed.

"I swear, nothing gets past anyone in this town," Tobias said with a laugh. "And don't you dare go using the L-word around Sally. At least not until I have a chance to say it first."

Iris crooned happily, but Summer dropped her bag to the ground with a large thud.

"Sorry," she stammered, bending down to gather it back up. "Did you say Sally? Sally Scott?"

"Yes, do you know her? We met at your wedding, actually."

She moved her bag from the floor to a small bistro table in the corner and crossed both arms over her chest before returning to stand before Tobias. "Maybe you did. But she wasn't my guest, and she really shouldn't have been there."

"Summer," her aunt warned. "Be nice."

Tobias startled at how quickly this woman went from happy to outright livid about his news. Why did she care so much, anyway? She was happily married to Ben Davis, and the whole town knew it.

Summer sighed. "You're right. I'm sorry," she mumbled to her aunt before turning back to him. "I'm not trying to be a downer, Tobias. It's just that Sally is the one person who never made me feel very welcome in this town."

Tobias shook his head. Sally had warned him that the townspeople didn't much care for her, but this was the first time he was seeing it for himself. "I'm sorry to hear that, but trust me. She's a nice person," he argued in Sally's defense. "Just a bit misunderstood."

"Well, I'm sure she's quite lovely," Iris said, motioning for Tobias to follow her toward the arrangements of flowers waiting in the cooler. "Now what flowers do you think we might like to surprise her with today?"

He turned to follow Iris, but Summer blocked his way. Her face was now red with fury. "You may be sure she's lovely, but *I'm sure* I didn't imagine her kissing my husband right before our wedding and asking him to run away with her!" She lowered both hands to her hips, ready for battle. Against whom, though, Tobias had no idea. There was no way shy, sweet Sally had tried to steal Summer's fiancé.

Iris rushed back toward her niece. "Summer, if you're going to harass my customers, you'll need to find somewhere else to work on your articles for the day." She pushed her toward the door, mouthing *sorry* to Tobias over her shoulder.

"I'm sorry about that," Iris repeated once Summer had been seen out. "She gets a little worked up sometimes."

"But why would she make something like that up? I don't get it."

Iris swallowed hard, unwilling to meet his eyes. "She's not making it up, Tobias. Ask her yourself, if you must, but it really did happen just as Summer said."

Tobias stood mute. How could this be true? It was so out of character for the Sally he knew. Until that weekend, he'd felt enormously guilty about keeping his secret from her, but had she also been keeping secrets? Was she still?

Iris shook her head and absentmindedly leafed through a giant binder on the counter. "Again I'm so sorry about that. Now let's take a look at those flowers, eh?"

"Actually, this is a bad idea," Tobias said, the words clawing his throat on the way out. "I'm sorry to have wasted your time."

As Tobias raced out of the shop and toward the library to ask Sally about what he'd just learned, he couldn't help but worry that he may have wasted his own time as well. He just hoped Sally would be able to explain everything.

FOURTEEN

S ally stared at the clock in the top right corner of her computer screen. The library had been painfully slow all afternoon. Normally that would be great because it would give her time to work on her novel. But ever since she'd received the texts from Tobias, she hadn't been able to focus on anything other than wondering what he had planned for the two of them that evening.

She watched as *4:32* became *4:33*. Just under an hour to go.

She tapped her pen on the edge of her desk, trying to will the seconds to tick faster.

A few painfully slow minutes later, the library doors slid open, admitting the first patron she'd seen in hours.

Sally smiled, thankful for the distraction. That is, until she saw just who was storming her way.

"Summer," she said, doing her best to keep her voice even and unaffected. "What brings you here today?"

"Is it true? Have you sunk your fangs into Tobias Lloyd now?" Summer placed both hands on the counter and leaned toward Sally, her normally composed manner completely absent.

Sally shook her head and wheeled her seat back to gain some distance. This wasn't the first time she'd been the subject of someone or another's rage, but it was the first time Summer had ever been anything but cordial. What had happened to change that?

"I don't know what you're talking about," she murmured as her stomach filled with dread. "I—"

"You know exactly what I'm talking about." Summer stomped around the desk and stared down at Sally from her towering position. "Tobias was just in my aunt's shop talking about how you two are crazy for each other, but that can't be right when you were just declaring your undying love for my husband not three months ago."

So this whole time, Summer had acted casual while her anger bubbled just beneath the surface, a coursing river of lava surging through her veins. But why now? So she ran into Tobias that afternoon. Why did Summer even care that the two of them were dating now?

Sally gulped, realizing now that she was trapped behind her desk. "I never got the chance to say sorry about that. It was a really rough time for me, and I—"

"*For you!* How do you think I felt? You never even bothered to apologize." Summer huffed and rolled her eyes, but stood her ground nonetheless. "Instead you act like I stole Ben away from you even though he was never interested in you to begin with. It's not right."

"I-I-I-I thought you'd be happy I moved on. Ben is just a friend. I've finally realized he wasn't the man for me. That somebody else is." If Summer didn't leave soon, Sally would throw up right on her shoes. She needed to get out of there, needed to find a way to escape, but Summer had her cornered.

"Ben is not your friend. Not anymore. How could you possibly think what you did was okay, that you're good enough for someone as nice as Tobias after what you did? *Unbelievable.*"

The door slid opened again, admitting a stunned Tobias who immediately charged over to insert himself in the scene.

Both women turned toward him, falling silent at once.

It was Tobias who spoke first. "What's going on here?" he demanded.

Sally pushed past Summer and rushed out from behind the desk. She crumpled into his arms, letting tears soil his checkered shirt.

"Summer?" Tobias asked as he stroked Sally's hair and held her close. "What happened? Why is Sally crying?"

For the first time since she'd entered the library, Summer's voice softened. "I saw you at the shop and I just got so angry. I needed her to know she'd hurt me."

"If she didn't know before, she definitely knows now. I think you should leave."

Sally clung even tighter to Tobias. Nobody had ever come to her rescue before, not like this. Aunt Fiona would if she were able to leave the house, and Ben used to stop others from talking bad about her, but Tobias seemed ready to go to war if he had to.

"She tried to kiss Ben!" Summer's fury had returned in full force. "She asked him to leave me at the altar and run away with her!"

"But Ben didn't go, and Sally hasn't made another pass at him since. Have you, sweetie?"

"*No,*" she mumbled into Tobias's shirt. Shame filled her heart, but still she couldn't let go of Tobias's strong arms. She needed him now more than ever.

Summer snorted. "And you better not again."

Tobias hugged Sally closer. *"There.* Will you please stop harassing her now and just go?"

"Tobias!" Summer shouted. "She's the one who—"

"Seriously, Summer, enough. Sally made a mistake, but she's sorry. She's moved on, and you should, too."

"Oh, Tobias." Summer let out a deep sigh before continuing. "Do you have any idea what you're getting into? Haven't you heard what people say about her? Haven't you noticed she hasn't got any friends? There's a reason for that."

"Whatever the case may be, I make my decisions for myself. And I, for one, think Sally is the best person in this entire town." Tobias bent down and kissed her on the forehead, but Sally still made no effort to let go.

She pictured Summer rolling her eyes, but didn't want to risk looking at her—especially since it seemed she was finally going to leave.

"Well, don't say I didn't warn you. And I hope you two will be very happy together."

Tobias hugged Sally even tighter as he said, "We already are."

* * *

Tobias watched as Summer finally turned on her heel and charged out of the library. Her curly hair bounced with each step until she disappeared through the sliding glass doors and back into the downtown area. This was definitely not how he'd pictured their evening going, but at least they were together now. And things could only get better from here.

Sally shook in his arms, letting out a big, wracking sob. "I'm so sorry!" she cried into his chest.

He reached for her face and tipped it up to look at his. "You have nothing to be sorry about. Summer should be apologizing to you after that horrible scene."

"But she's right," Sally insisted with a sniffle. "I did tell Ben I loved him. I did try to kiss him before the wedding. I couldn't let him get married without knowing. I thought it would make things easier, but it only made everything so much worse."

"Stop that right now." He glanced around the library and found that the two of them were completely alone. This wasn't how he'd initially planned to share the depth of his feelings with Sally, but the time had come—and she needed to know. "I don't care who you loved before. All I care is who you love now. Do you love me, Sally?"

She swiped at her eyes, but the redness remained. "What?"

"Do you love me?" he repeated, offering her a reassuring smile as he did.

"So much," she confessed after sucking in a deep breath. "So much that it scares me."

"Then we'll be brave together," Tobias said, catching a tear as it rolled down her cheek. "Because I love you, too."

Sally laughed through her tears. "This is not the scene I imagined saying those three little words for the first time, but I'm glad we said them."

He shrugged playfully, fixing his eyes on her soft pink lips. "Well, we do things differently, you and I, and that's okay. May I kiss you now?"

She nodded, and he brought his lips to hers, allowing them to linger as long as he felt she needed him. When at last Sally pushed gently on his chest, Tobias tucked her hair behind her ears and smiled. "I came early because I couldn't wait to see you. I have exciting news."

"Oh?" Sally reluctantly left his arms and grabbed a tissue from the box on her desk. "What's that?" she asked, trying to discreetly wipe her nose.

"I found the perfect location for my firm," he revealed hardly able to contain his growing excitement. "Well, actually, you did."

"Me?" He watched as recognition lit her eyes. "You mean Fred's old pizza place?"

"I mean Tobias's new law place, but yes. I'm ready to sign the lease, but first I needed my lucky charm at my side." He frowned, realizing how insensitive he was being by expecting Sally to be in the mood to celebrate after that big fight with Summer. "If you don't feel up to it tonight, though, I'll understand."

"That sounds like the perfect way to spend the evening." She tossed her used tissue in the basket and rubbed some hand sanitizer into her palms before grabbing hold of Tobias's hand and asking, "A-are you sure you aren't mad about Ben?"

Mad? How could he ever be mad when he had the love of the most wonderful woman he'd ever met? Tobias twirled Sally into his arms. "Hey, he missed his chance. I think I owe him a thank you for that."

She laughed before turning serious again. "Well, now you know one of my secrets. You may as well find out the other tonight, too."

"Another secret? Sally Scott, you are a woman of many surprises."

She smiled sweetly. "This one isn't a secret on purpose. I've just never had many friends, so I've never had much of a reason to invite people over. Tobias, will you come and meet my aunt Fiona?"

Tobias thought back to a few months ago when

he'd tried to look Sally up on Facebook and found Fiona instead. She never did accept his friend request, but now she didn't need to. They'd be meeting in real life instead. He loved that Sally had invited him to meet her family but also wondered why she hadn't spoken much about them before.

"I'd love that," he said, truly meaning it. "And I hope that I'm much, much more than a friend by now."

Sally giggled shyly, the gap between her teeth on full display. "Yes, I guess you are."

"You guess? How can I make you sure?" he asked with a mischievous grin he reserved only for Sally.

"Tell me you love me again?" she asked with a delicate shrug and a giant grin.

"I love you again," he joked.

Sally fixed him with a glare that could turn any man into stone, so he quickly added, "And I love you always."

Somehow he knew he would. No matter where life took him next, his heart would always belong with Sally.

FIFTEEN

Nobody had ever considered Sally lucky before. Few had even found her helpful. Yet here Tobias was, insisting she kiss the pen he would soon use to sign the lease for his firm's new location.

"It is a shame, though," the middle-aged realtor said, shaking her head. Sally had seen her around town but never gotten to know the older woman. She hadn't gotten to know much of anyone, but especially not those who couldn't be bothered to visit the library every now and again. "I really thought Fred was going to make it. He sure will be missed around here."

Sally wedged her fingers between each of Tobias's on his right hand while he used his left to sign the contract. "I'm sure Fred will enjoy his retirement. But now it's Tobias's turn to make his mark on Sweet Grove."

Tobias finished signing with a flourish and then filled out a check, which he offered the realtor. "I can't believe it's really mine," he said, his eyes widening as he gazed around the empty storefront.

"Congratulations," the realtor said, collecting the paperwork and then giving each of their hands a firm shake. The location had sat vacant for the last few months after Fred's closing, and cobwebs had started to settle in the corners. The realtor was probably beside herself for being able to lease the property again so soon given that so few new people moved to town and everyone who was already here knew all about the alleged curse.

Tobias didn't care, though, and neither did Sally. She was simply overjoyed that he'd be staying here in Sweet Grove with her. First they'd build up his business, and then they could make their life together. All the pieces were clicking perfectly into place.

Together they watched the real estate broker leave the building and get into her hulking SUV out front. When she'd finally driven off, Tobias grabbed Sally by the waist and spun her around. They both laughed and kissed and danced, enjoying each other's company and celebrating this big step toward the future.

"I never thought I'd be so excited about someone putting down roots in Sweet Grove," Sally admitted on the drive back to the library where they planned to pick up her car before heading home in separate vehicles to meet her aunt.

Tobias frowned. "Yeah, well, things are going to be different now. You're my girl, and I'll make sure everyone knows it."

"That's sweet, Tobias, but you don't have to do that. There are a lot of years of history that just can't be erased. I don't mind, though, because now I'm finally starting to feel like I belong. At least in my own small little corner." She loved that he wanted to fight for her, but at the same time, she longed to be done fighting. If it meant smiling and waving at the neighbors, if it meant swallowing her tongue from time to time and volunteering to run the Fall Festival, then that's what she would do.

Tobias didn't seem to like that, though. "But you shouldn't have to be stuck in a corner. The whole world should be yours. The stars, too."

"Okay, now you're just being ridiculous. And corny." Sally laughed so hard she had to stop in order to breathe again.

Tobias fake-pouted even though he'd joined in the laughter as well. "It's a good thing you're the writer, huh?"

"It would certainly seem so." She gave him

another kiss before unbuckling her seatbelt and heading to her own car. It wasn't far, so they both agreed Tobias would follow Sally over rather than plugging the address into his phone's GPS.

Sure enough, three minutes later, they stood hand-in-hand on her doorstep. "Are you ready?" Sally asked, looking up at Tobias for an indication of how he was feeling in that moment.

He still wore the same euphoric expression he'd donned when signing the lease. In fact, he was rarely without a smile these days. "Ready and excited. Let's do this."

Sally took a deep breath and opened the door. She'd told her aunt everything about Tobias, but he knew practically nothing about her. She also didn't know he'd be coming home with Sally that evening. Sure, she could have texted to let her aunt know, but the pending visit would only spike her anxiety. Surprises, while not appreciated, were always preferred when it came to Aunt Fiona.

"Hello!" Sally called into the empty house, wondering where her aunt could possibly be. Normally she sat waiting in her chair for Sally to return from work, but the living room lay dark and bare.

Spooky trotted over and rubbed himself up

against the leg of Tobias's khakis. He bent down to pet the happy feline as Sally continued to search the lower level without any luck.

"You stay here with Spooky, and I'll go see if I can find my aunt," Sally said, trying not to show how afraid she felt in that moment. Her aunt never left the house. *Never.*

So where could she possibly be?

Sally thought over the alternatives in her mind. Either Aunt Fiona was lying injured and unresponsive somewhere in the house, or someone had forced her out of it.

"Aunt Fiona!" Sally called, climbing the stairs two at a time now. Once upstairs, she peered into her aunt's bedroom, but it, too, was empty.

At last she noticed a fog of steam rising from beneath the bathroom door, and Sally took a deep sigh of relief.

She knocked on the door and called her aunt's name, but was greeted only by a sniffle. Trying to twist the knob open, she found that it wasn't locked so she knocked again and gently cracked the door open.

A wall of steam hit her in the face. It took her a moment to see through into the shower where she found her aunt sitting on the floor of the tub fully dressed as the pounding water rolled off her in rivulets.

"Aunt Fiona!" Sally cried. "What happened?"

Her aunt looked up at her with reddened eyes, shivering violently despite the heat that flooded the room. "Sally," she moaned. "He got married. He had kids."

"Who? Who got married and had kids?"

"Al. Remember my boyfriend from before? He made me choose, and I knew I'd chosen right so I never looked back. But then after our talk, I looked him up on Facebook and saw he has this whole big family now. It wasn't that he didn't want kids, Sally. *He didn't want me.*"

* * *

Tobias waited with Sally's very affectionate black cat as she searched the house for her aunt. He could hear the rising panic in her voice each new time she called out Fiona's name, but Tobias stayed put as he'd been told. As one minute became two, he debated going off in search of Sally himself.

But then his phone buzzed impatiently in his pocket.

Noting that it was just his grandfather, he sent the

call through to voicemail. He'd be home soon enough and could check in with him then. But no sooner had he placed his phone back into his pocket then it started to ring again.

"What is it, Gramps?" he asked, putting the phone to his ear and hoping this call would be quick in case Sally and her aunt needed him.

"Sir, this isn't your grandfather," an unfamiliar voice answered. "My name is Collins. I'm an EMT for the county and wanted to call you before we took your grandfather in to St. Joseph's. I saw you were the only number he ever called, so figured that made you his ICE."

The unfamiliar acronyms swirled around Tobias's head. The only thing he knew for sure was that his grandfather was in trouble and that it was his job to get to him ASAP.

"ICE?" he mumbled into the receiver, panic mounting. "What? What happened to Gramps? Where are you?"

A series of loud thumps sounded on the other end of the line before the paramedic spoke again. "He's unconscious. We think it may have been a heart attack but won't know for sure until we get him in. We've just got him loaded into the ambulance. Can you meet us at the hospital?"

"I'm headed there now." Tobias hung up the

phone, realizing he'd need to say goodbye to Sally before he raced to his grandfather's aid. He kicked off his shoes out of respect for the pristinely kept house and his new girlfriend before jogging up the stairs.

Sally met him halfway down. "I'm afraid we have to cancel tonight," she said with a vacant expression.

"I was just going to tell you the same thing." He stumbled back down the stairs and jammed his shoes onto his feet. "My gramps had a heart attack. Well, maybe. I don't know exactly what happened yet, but I have to go to him."

"My aunt is having a hard time tonight, too. She needs me." Sally joined him by the door and wrapped her arms around him, sobbing gently into his shoulder. He wished he could stay and comfort her, but his grandfather needed him more in that moment.

"You have my love and my prayers. I'll call you as soon as I can." With a quick kiss, he was out the door.

Didn't we just do this? Tobias wondered as he sped through the streets of Sweet Grove. Sherriff Grant would understand, but Tobias hoped he wouldn't need to explain himself for going at least ten over and skipping a stop sign or two. Time was of the essence. His grandmother had died before she ever made it to the hospital. What if his gramps did the same? What if it was already too late?

He tried to picture Sally's smile rather than his Gramp's curved posture and spotted hands. Tears burned at his eyes, and he let them fall freely. Because how could he ever hope to make a future if he lost everything important from his past?

"Please be okay. Please be okay," he prayed, letting the repetition of the words wipe his mind clean. When at last he reached the hospital, he was let straight through to ER.

Apparently, his grandfather had arrived only minutes earlier and still hadn't regained consciousness by the time Tobias found him. A team of medical personnel arrived and began checking his vitals while the paramedics shared their updates from the ride over.

"He's in acute adrenal failure," someone said. "We need to get him to the ICU!"

"Wait!" Tobias cried as they wheeled his grandfather away on the gurney. "Wait!"

"I'm sorry, son," an older doctor told him. "We'll give you an update as soon as we can."

Tobias stood rooted to the spot as the one person who had always been there for him was taken away. Would he ever see him again? If Gramps woke up, would he still be the same man Tobias loved more than life itself? How could he possibly weather life's storms without his anchor? His savior? His grandpa?

"C'mon, honey," a nurse said, placing an arm around Tobias's shoulder and leading him back to the waiting room as he wept openly and unapologetically.

Oh, Sally, he thought. *I hope your night is going better than mine.*

SIXTEEN

Sally helped Aunt Fiona out of the tub and into a dry set of pajamas and a warm robe. She hadn't seen her like this in years—not since the last time she'd tried to leave the house and failed miserably.

"Would you like me to make you some tea?" Sally asked, unsure of what other comfort she could offer for this particular crisis.

Aunt Fiona shook her head, then scooted down in bed and pulled the covers over her head. From the new shape the blanket took, Sally could tell her aunt had grabbed her knees and brought them up to her chest in the classic panic position.

"I don't know how to help you," Sally admitted softly as she crossed the room to pull the curtains closed. "You said you chose me over Al. You said you never regretted it."

But when she turned back toward the lumpy form on the bed, she realized then how much her aunt's episode was hurting her, too. She'd never blamed herself for her aunt's condition before, but perhaps she should have. After all, it was Sally who had turned her life on end, taken away the one man she'd ever loved and ultimately had burdened the older woman so much that Fiona had decided she'd rather shut life out than attempting to live it anymore.

Her aunt said nothing—just sobbed and shook beneath the blanket.

Sally waited for her to apologize, to say she loved Sally and didn't regret their life together, but the words didn't come.

Shaking with fury, Sally stalked across the room and ripped the covers off her aunt. She'd been annoyed by her condition before, but never angry. Not like now.

"Snap out of it!" she shouted, even though she knew from support group that this was the worst thing she could say. At this moment, however, it felt like the only thing she could say, so she said it again. "Snap out of it! Stop with this pity party! Just get better already!"

Her aunt grew still before slowly unfurling her limbs and craning her neck in the direction of her niece. Sally's anger had apparently sobered her because she sat up and spoke to her in a level voice. "I can't get magically better, Sally. Agoraphobia doesn't work that way. Neither does depression. And, unfortunately, I've got both."

That's when it came at last. The guilt Sally should have felt at even thinking the words, let alone screaming them at her aunt, now filled her heart.

"I know," she said, looking away so she wouldn't have to see her aunt's crumpled face and weak, defeated body. "I know. I shouldn't have said that. I'm sorry."

"I can't get magically better," Fiona repeated as she stared at her empty lap. "But you can."

"What?" Sally sank onto the bed, dizzy from the rapid turns in this conversation.

Fiona reached for Sally and pulled her into her side. They both sat against the tall, plush headboard while Fiona continued to cry silently. "As much as I know you don't want to hear it," she said between gentle sobs, "you're normal, you're healthy. The only thing holding you back is you... and me."

Sally laid her head on her aunt's shoulder, just like she'd done since she was a five-year-old girl. But now she was bigger than her aunt, taller, stronger—and just as helpless as ever. "Aunt Fiona, no. Stop it. I love you. We need each other. We're a team."

Her aunt shook her head and forced a smile. "I need you, but you don't need me. You'd be better off without me, and we both know that's a fact."

The fear returned. Her aunt didn't talk like this. Even though they'd always stayed in their own little world together in that old house, they'd always been happy. But now it almost sounded as if Aunt Fiona wished she were dead. Would she take her own life like Ben's brother had? Sally needed to figure it out and fast. She couldn't lose her dear aunt, and she also couldn't let her suffer. Not like this.

"Why are you saying this now?" she cried. "How could you think I would ever leave you?"

Her aunt's voice became scratchy despite all the tears. "Because I don't want what happened to me to happen to you, Sally. I don't regret my choice. I've never regretted choosing you, but the other day, hearing about how you're falling in love... You can't have it both ways, Sally."

"Of course I can," she argued. "Tobias is a good man. He understands the importance of family. He would never—"

"Listen to me." Fiona let go of Sally and struggled to her feet as if the added height would give her words added power, too. "You're normal and you deserve to live a normal life. It's been hard enough on you already. You've gone through too much from too young an age, but finally you can be happy."

"I am happy. Aunt Fiona, look at me. I'm happy. Stop saying I'm not."

Her aunt turned to face Sally again, her eyes red and scary. She almost didn't recognize her. "I shouldn't have told you about Al. I'm so stupid. I shouldn't have made you think—"

"Stop telling me what I think! And don't tell me what I feel! I can love Tobias, and I can love you, and I can still love Ben as a friend. You don't have to give up one person to let in another."

Fiona's entire body shook as if possessed, then she fell forward onto the bed, wailing as she did. Sally didn't know what to do, but she couldn't ignore this breakdown and hope her aunt's brain mended itself. So she sang her favorite song from all the way back when Aunt Fiona had been healthy and the two of them had gone to First Street Church every Sunday morning.

"This little light of mine," she sang as best as she could through tears. "I'm gonna let it shine."

Tobias poured himself another cup of the cheap vending machine coffee and waited for any news of his grandfather. Sally called at one point to tell him she didn't feel comfortable leaving her aunt that night, but that she could stay on the phone with him while he waited at the hospital.

They talked for a while, but both of their hearts hung heavy with worry, making the conversation forced and ultimately bringing it to an early end. Tobias hated himself in that moment. He couldn't be there for Sally in her time of need and he hadn't been there for Gramps, either.

The whole point of moving back to Sweet Grove and opening his own practice was to help look after his grandfather. Yet he'd spent every free moment either with Sally or thinking about Sally, leaving his poor grandfather to get even sicker than he'd been to begin with. Now what would happen?

He had hours to contemplate that very question as he sat alone in the waiting room, but no good answer presented itself.

Finally, after what felt like years and years, a doctor came to speak to him. Tobias sent up a quick prayer of gratitude when he realized the man in scrubs didn't wear the grim expression that implied bad news was on its way.

Instead he looked tired, tired but hopeful. "Your grandfather is awake. We've started an IV and he's doing much better."

After they shook hands, Tobias didn't know what to do with his, so he crossed his arms over his chest and began to sway on his feet. He had almost no strength left after today, but he needed to find a little more—at least enough to learn what he could do to help poor Gramps. "Was it a heart attack like the paramedic said?"

The doctor shook his head and looked down at the chart in his hands. "No, his heart is weak, but what he suffered today was an addisonian crisis."

"I don't understand." Tobias considered himself an educated man, but he'd never heard of this particular disease before. Was it something rare and difficult to treat? Would his grandfather actually be okay, or was the doctor simply masking the truth with his neutral expression? Tobias needed to know, and he needed to know now.

"He had an acute adrenal failure from leaving his Addison's Disease untreated."

Tobias shook his head. How was this possible? "Addison's Disease? That's the first time I'm hearing of it. Does Gramps know he has it?"

"Yes, he was here back in the spring when he

received his diagnosis. Addison's is very treatable, but only if the patient keeps up on his medication."

This was not what he'd expected to hear. The fact that Gramps had kept this from him and willfully ignored the doctor's instructions hurt him deeply. "So what now?" he asked the doctor.

"We'll keep him for a couple days. Make sure he's okay and that his levels return to normal. When he heads home, he has to keep up on his medication, though. We'd also like you to take his blood pressure each day, if you can. If it drops below ninety over sixty, give us a call so we can decide next steps."

"Next steps? Is my grandfather going to die?" He uncrossed his arms and wracked both hands through his hair. This could not be happening. Not now. Not ever.

The doctor clapped a hand on Tobias's back and offered a fleeting smile that did little to reassure him. "Not for a very long time if we can help it. I'll send a nurse to get you once he's ready for visitors."

Tobias thanked the doctor and sat back down in the waiting room, pulling up Web MD on his phone to read about his grandfather's diagnosis. Why hadn't Gramps told him about this, and why had he stopped taking his medicine? It just didn't make any sense. Did Gramps want to die? Did he simply forget to take his medicine, or was his mind starting to go, too?

Tobias hated thinking of his grandfather as anything but a survivor, a nurturer, a friend.

Yet here he was, laid up in the hospital and undergoing emergency treatment.

All the articles he read online said that Addison's could be fatal but often wasn't—especially with regular treatment. But his grandfather had already proven he couldn't take care of himself. How could Tobias possibly expect to start his own firm, settle down with Sally and start a family, and keep after his grandfather and his beloved restaurant?

Some very big sacrifices would need to be made —and soon.

His grandparents had willingly given up so much to be there for Tobias when his mother had decided she didn't want him. In fact, Tobias owed his very life to them. So how could he turn his back on his grandfather now when the old man was most vulnerable?

No matter how much it hurt, something else would have to go in order to make space for the daily care and checkups Gramps would need. His law practice could wait while he helped run the restaurant.

But what about Sally?

He couldn't ask her to wait indefinitely.

Did that mean he would have to let her go, too?

SEVENTEEN

Sally awoke the next morning alone in her aunt's bed, despite falling asleep with Fiona beside her. The sound of movement in the kitchen forced her to her feet. She was still too tired to form any cohesive thoughts yet, until she opened the door and the smell of sizzling bacon filled her nostrils.

Sure enough, her aunt stood in front of the stove making breakfast with a blank expression on her face.

"Good morning," Sally said around a yawn. "How are you feeling?"

"Everything's always better by the light of day," Aunt Fiona answered right on cue as she moved the strips of meat around the pan.

Sally recognized this platitude from one of her aunt's online support groups, which could mean almost anything. What she really wanted to know, though, was if this was the calm after the storm or merely the eye of the hurricane. Was her aunt truly on the mend now or simply holding the grief beneath the surface until it overtook her once more?

"Do you want to talk about last night?" Sally ventured carefully, trying to appear more at ease than she felt.

"I'll be fine," her aunt promised with a gentle shake of her head as she kept her eyes glued on the frying pan. "I just hadn't thought of Al in a long time and I hadn't given myself time to grieve our relationship. It was a long time coming is all."

Sally raised one eyebrow in suspicion. "Are you sure?"

Fiona's voice brightened. She wore a smile now. "Yes, totally sure. I even deleted my Facebook so I wouldn't be tempted to look him up again."

Sally chose not to mention how easy it was to *un*delete social media accounts. It was why she'd never signed up for them in the first place—that and she didn't need another reminder of how few friends she had in this world. "Well, that's a start," she said.

"I already called Doctor Sara, by the way," Fiona continued. "She's coming over later this morning to talk."

"Do you want me to be here for that?"

Her aunt smiled and shook her head. "Nope, I need to learn to take care of myself. It's high time."

Sally sighed. So even after that huge argument last night, they'd gotten nowhere. "We take care of each other. It's what we've always done."

"But it doesn't have to be what we do forever. You're a grown up, Sally. You need your own life." She poured a glass of orange juice and took a long, slow drink. "Besides, I survived when you were in college, didn't I?"

College. Those had been some of the tensest years of Sally's life, not just because she accelerated her studies to complete her bachelor's in three years instead of the recommended four, but also knowing her aunt was all alone with no one to keep her company. They talked on the phone every night, but Sally knew it hadn't been enough. Fiona knew it, too, so why was she trying so hard to push Sally away again?

"Let's try not to make any big decisions today," Sally offered peaceably.

"I'm not deciding anything. I'm just letting you know it's okay to move on. My sickness isn't your sickness, and I love you too much to keep holding you back."

"Okay. Thanks, Aunt Fiona," Sally said dismissively.

"I know you don't mean it, but you will thank me later." Her aunt finished at the stove and took a seat beside her at the counter. "Unfinished business isn't just for ghosts, you know. Like with me and Al, I let that fester for years rather than dealing with it in a healthy way like I should've. I know you have regrets, too. Things that are unresolved."

Sally broke into her egg yolk and smeared it around the plate while she listened to her aunt's words.

"You're great at hiding." Fiona stopped to chuckle. "Hey, you learned from the best!" She sobered again and turned toward Sally in the stool. Her eyes searched Sally's as she continued. "But I really do think you should tie up your loose ends around here and then decide what you really want out of life. I doubt it's living locked in this house until we both die and Spooky eats our rotting corpses."

Sally pushed her plate away. That particular image stole the hunger right out of her belly. "Ewww, Aunt Fiona. Gross."

"Just trying to lighten the mood a bit. But please, think about what I said." Fiona turned her stool back toward the counter, apparently having no difficulty eating herself. After she took a bite of toast, she mumbled softly, "Maybe pray about it, too?"

That took Sally by surprise. As much as the two shared with each other over the years, faith wasn't one of those things. "Pray? I didn't think you believed in God anymore."

"Why wouldn't I believe in God? Oh, right, because my sister died, my world got turned upside down, and I stopped going to church. Well… yeah, that's on me, but I still pray every day. Read my Bible, too."

"So you believe in God after everything?" Sally couldn't believe it. If anyone had a reason to doubt God, it was Fiona.

But her aunt was insistent. "Of course, I've needed Him more than ever these last few… okay, twenty years. Do you not believe in God anymore, Sally?"

"I honestly don't know. It's not like believing has helped you out. No offense."

Her aunt chuckled softly. "None of us are perfect. It's why we need Him."

"Maybe." Sally continued to play with her food, pushing it all into a pile in the center of her plate.

"Not maybe. *Definitely.* No wonder you feel so lost."

"I'm not lost. I know exactly where I belong.

Here. With you." Sally didn't like where this conversation was headed. It felt odd discussing these things with her aunt—or at all.

"That's just an excuse, baby girl, and you know it. Regardless, it's time you figured things out. And it's time we stopped enabling each other."

Was Sally's aunt blaming her for her sickness? Was she suggesting that Sally, too, harbored great ills? She didn't like either possible answer. "What do you mean by that?" she demanded.

Fiona shrugged, much more at ease in this conversation than her niece. "I don't know yet. Maybe it's time I finally got help."

"But *I* help you," Sally insisted. She felt like the chopped liver cat food they fed Spooky on vet days. "The doctors. The medicines. We're doing all we can, and you're happy, aren't you?"

Fiona turned in her stool again and offered a sad smile. "Of course I'm happy, but I'm worried that you're not."

* * *

Tobias stayed by his grandfather's side for the next two days as they waited for the all clear from the hospital staff. Sally came to visit for a brief period each day to support Tobias more than his grandfather. Every time he saw her, his heart seized. What had he done to earn this broken angel, and how could he keep deserving her while also making sure his gramps stayed healthy and well looked after?

This whole incident brought many things into focus. From that first moment the EMT had called, Tobias had dropped everything to be with Gramps, which worked out fine this time, but he wouldn't be able to take such flexible leave once his firm opened and he had clients depending on him. Besides, did he really want that much responsibility on his shoulders? Was he ready for it?

One thing he was definitely not ready for was the visitor he and Gramps received during their last afternoon in the hospital.

Anna Lloyd.

If not for her frequent social media posts, Tobias wouldn't have recognized the lanky, fair-haired woman as his own mother. Yet here she was now, breezing into the room like she owned the place. She gave Tobias a quick hug, the kind where you didn't even close your arms all the way. Still, it was too much for Tobias who now felt tainted by this fake expression of endearment.

"How is he doing?" she asked Tobias with a quick glance around the room.

The toilet flushed and the door to Gramps's

private bathroom swung open before Tobias had a chance to answer.

"He is doing just fine. Thanks," the old man grumbled.

"Here, let me." She rushed to his side and grabbed his elbow to help him toward the bed, but Gramps shook her off.

"I told you not to come," he barked with anger the likes of which Tobias had rarely seen before.

Tobias and his mother both watched as Ernie settled himself back in bed.

"But I love you and wanted to make sure you were okay," she argued.

"I have Tobias, so I'm fine. And I'm not changing my will, no matter how many little visits you decide to pay me."

"Daddy, be reasonable. I don't need your money. Joe has more than enough to look after us both. To look after you, too, if you need it."

Joe—that was the new husband, Tobias remembered. Where was he? Why wasn't he here with his wife when her father was presumably on his death bed? It seemed that maybe Anna's life hadn't worked out quite like she planned, after all.

The old man turned in his bed, unwilling to look at his daughter a moment longer. "Nope, no thank you. And goodbye."

For a moment, Tobias actually felt sorry for her. He'd lost his mother, but she'd lost both parents because of her decision to leave.

She looked so defeated now but still wouldn't take no for an answer. "I flew all this way to—"

"And you can fly right on back," Ernie told her coldly. *"Auf wiedersehen."*

"Fine, if that's how you want it," she said with a sigh, waiting for only a moment before turning on heel to leave.

Tobias followed his mother out of the hospital room and placed a hand on her shoulder. "Wait. Why did you come?"

She turned around with fresh tears in her eyes. "To see my father, but I guess that's off the table."

They regarded each other curiously before Tobias spoke again. "Do you love him? Do you love Gramps?" he asked.

"Of course I do. He's my dad."

"But…" He didn't know what he could possibly say, so he let the meek word trail away.

"How can I be capable of love when I never loved you?" She surprised him by reading his thoughts despite the limited amount of time they'd spent together over the years.

He buried his hands deep into his pockets and forced himself to maintain eye contact.

181

"Actually, yeah, that's exactly what I want to know."

"Let's go grab a coffee," she said, continuing back down the hall. "I can tell this is going to be a long talk."

Tobias followed her to the bustling hospital cafeteria, not saying another word until they were both settled with steaming cups before them.

"I'm really messed up, because of you," he stated factually. This could be his only chance to confront her face to face, which meant it wasn't the time to mince words.

Rather than apologizing or even showing any sign of guilt, his mother laughed. "Is that so? Because the man I see sitting before me is handsome, kind, smart, and about to open his own law firm. That's not a mess by many people's definitions."

"But you didn't want me. You..." He dropped his voice to a whisper. "You tried to abort me."

Anna shook her head sadly. "No, not you. A baby I had never met. I was ten years younger than you are now, imagine. I was scared. I never wanted to be a mom, and I thought it would be better for everyone, if..." She let her words fade away, and neither bothered to finish them.

They sat in tense silence as they both took sips from their coffees.

It was Anna who spoke next. "Once you were born, I knew it with even greater certainty. I was never meant to be a mom, and you'd be better off without me. Looks like I was right, by the way."

"But you said you hated me. You said I ruined your life." He hated that he had to remind her of these things. They had happened. He was not crazy, and he was not misremembering. In fact, the very memory of those words had been etched so deeply into his brain that he'd never be able to erase them, no matter how hard he tried.

"Yeah, I did say those things. I was young and emotional, and I'm sorry if I hurt you. But I'm not sorry I've stayed out of your life. It's what we both needed."

There was one question he needed answered above all else, so he took a deep, shaky breath and asked, "Are you sorry I was born?"

"I was back then, but now I'm glad you're here to take care of Dad. He obviously loves you very much."

"And I love him, too."

They both fell silent. Neither said they loved the other because they both knew that wasn't true. And, for the first time in his life, Tobias took it for what it was. Not a failure on his part, but rather hers. He didn't need to prove anything to her because nothing would ever be enough to change her mind.

Life didn't always go according to plan, but it carried on just the same.

"Well, I better go see about changing up my flight," his mother said, rising to stand and offering him a lingering smile before leaving their table.

Tobias remained seated as she walked away.

EIGHTEEN

Sally had given her aunt's words a lot of thought but still felt lost. *Was* she unhappy? Did she need something more in her life to be fulfilled? She'd tried whispering her thoughts to God in the still of the night but felt silly every time.

After a great deal of back and forth without landing on any real answers, she decided to write out her thoughts and see if that could provide the clarity she craved.

After all, it had always been easier for her to open up via written words rather than those that were spoken. Perhaps a letter to God would take that hesitation away. It was certainly worth a try.

And so she opened a blank Word document on her computer and began to type:

Dearest Creator,
It is with great uncertainty, I—

Sally laughed to herself and hit the backspace key several times. She would never feel close to God if she approached talking to him so formally. She needed to say what was in her heart, pure and simple, with no added frills.

And so she began again:

God,

I used to believe in you, and I want to again. Here's the thing: it's hard to believe in a magnanimous creator when there's so much suffering all around us. My parents died. Aunt Fiona can't leave the house. I haven't spoken with my best friend in months. And I just don't know what's next for me.

But you do, right?

Please guide me in what comes next, because I can't do it alone.

Amen,
Sally Scott

Satisfied now, she printed the paper, folded it up, and stuck it deep in her pocket. It seemed like it might get answered faster if she carried it around with her, like that would add extra emphasis to her prayer.

She cleared her document and started a new letter:

Summer,

> *I want to say I'm sorry—*

Sally stopped typing and let out a deep sigh. This was one she needed to do live and in person. No typing out her thoughts this time. After all, this apology was long overdue.

"Aunt Fiona!" she called up the stairs. "I'm going out for a little while. I'll be back in time for evening tea!"

Before her aunt could answer, she slid her feet into her favorite pair of sandals and bolted out the door. Aunt Fiona had taken to doing more activities independently these past few days. She still stayed at home, but she spent more and more time in her room, listened to audiobooks without Sally, and did other little things on her own to show her niece that she was fine—and that she'd continue to be fine if Sally decided to move on.

Of course, Sally didn't like that one bit, but Aunt Fiona had been right about at least one thing. She needed to take care of some unfinished business. She drove to Ben's house, hoping she'd find both him and his wife there.

The newlyweds had decided to move in with his mother to help oversee her recovery after a lengthy stint in rehab. That was another reason why Sally had always identified so closely with Ben: they both knew what it was like to have to now care for the women who'd taken care of them as children.

Taking a deep breath and doing her best to resist the urge to run, Sally lifted her hand to the door and knocked.

"Coming!" Summer called from the other side. A moment later the door swung open... and then shut again almost just as fast.

"Summer, wait!" Sally pleaded through the thick wood. "I'm here to see *you*."

The door opened just the slightest crack, revealing a sliver of Summer's face as she said, "Me?"

"Yes, I owe you an apology. I..." Sally felt silly pouring her heart out when she could barely even see Summer's face, and where any passersby could easily overhear their conversation. "Can I come in?"

Summer nodded and opened the door the rest of the way. "Ben's not here," she said, eyeing the other woman with trepidation.

"He doesn't need to be." Sally stepped inside and took her shoes off by the door. "Perhaps it's best if he's not."

"If you're sure." Summer led Sally into the small kitchen and motioned for her to sit. "Water?" she asked.

"No, I'm fine," Sally said, realizing only then that her throat was parched. But never mind that—she needed to get the words out before they consumed her from within.

"Summer," she began once the other woman had taken a seat across from her. "I'm so sorry for everything. I'm sorry I was mean to you when you were new in town, that I was jealous of you and Ben, that I tried to kiss him and get him to call off your wedding, and that it took me so long to realize I owe you an apology."

The other woman kept her gaze focused on the scratched table top, but Sally thought she caught the beginnings of a frown. "So why are you saying all of this now?"

"Because I've realized that leaving problems unresolved only causes them to get bigger, to hurt more. I'm really sorry I hurt you."

Summer risked a glance up. She studied Sally's face for a moment as if to assess her sincerity before finally offering a hesitant smile and saying, "You're right. About the problems growing, you're right. At first, I was so focused on the wedding that I didn't have time to process how I felt about what happened with you and Ben, but then once everything had settled down, I got angry. And each week that went by without an apology only made me angrier."

Sally nodded. She hadn't known Summer was hurting until their confrontation in the library. But of course she'd been. Summer was a genuinely nice person. She'd tried to be kind to Sally so many times, but Sally had never accepted her friendly overtures, and she'd fought as hard as she could to avoid any time spent in her company—even going so far as to refuse a direct request from her boss about planning the Fall Festival.

"I'm sorry," Sally said again. Now that the words were out there, it felt like she couldn't say them enough. With each new apology, she felt the burden of her guilt lighten. "I should have apologized sooner. I shouldn't have made a move on Ben to begin with. It's very obvious how much he loves you, then and now."

"Thank you. I accept your apology." Summer reached over and squeezed Sally's hand before quickly letting go again. "And I'm sorry, too, about the scene at the library the other day."

"It's okay. I deserved it," Sally muttered. There were many things Sally had deserved. The one that never made sense to her was Tobias. Why would he want her, and how would she ever be worthy of him?

Summer also seemed to have something more on her mind. Sure enough, she leaned forward and said, "Can I ask you a question?"

"Sure."

"Do you really love Tobias now?" She smiled again, and Sally felt the guilt creeping back in. All those times she'd cast Summer as the villain in her life and she'd never taken the chance to really look at her, to even try to get to know her. And now with Tobias, she'd let him in but was still afraid to go deeper.

"I really do, but I'm scared."

Summer tilted her head and offered a quizzical gaze.

"I'm scared he's too good for me," Sally clarified. It felt good to open up about this. It felt great talking to Summer as a friend instead of an adversary. "That it can't last."

Summer laughed good-naturedly. "That feeling doesn't ever totally go away. You just have to have faith in your partner and faith in God."

"I feel like everyone is saying that to me lately."

"Well, maybe that's because it's something you really need to hear," Summer suggested.

Just then Sally remembered the note in her pocket, the prayer to God. He'd already answered it, sending guidance in the form of her former enemy. That was the thing about relationships—they changed and grew. Some faded away over time, but as long as you chose to have faith, anything was possible.

At last Tobias's grandfather was given the clean bill of health and allowed to return home to his regular routine plus a few important modifications, like taking his medication. It seemed that a lifetime had passed in those few short days, and now that they were expected to return to normal, Tobias had a hard time discerning just what *normal* might mean.

He continued to put the work for his new law firm on hold so that he could help his grandfather hire a couple new full-time staffers for the restaurant. One of them was none other than Fred, the failed pizza man and his grandfather's former nemesis. Even though Gramps complained, Fred made perfect sense as an experienced restaurateur and someone with lots of time on his hands.

Thankfully, once Fred agreed not to change the menu in any way, Ernie let up on his protests. Tobias, for his part, tried not to mention the location of his new law firm, feeling immensely guilty, almost as if he had put the old man out of business himself.

Besides, he still didn't know what he wanted his future to look like.

Everything became even more topsy-turvy when he received a call from a former professor claiming she had the perfect job opportunity for him. Apparently she was leaving academia behind to open her own firm in the big city, and she wanted Tobias to join her as a junior partner. The salary was generous, and the offer was truly a once-in-a-lifetime kind of deal. But saying yes would mean leaving Gramps behind yet again. And what about Sally? Could he really ask her to leave her aunt, job, and entire life behind to follow him to the city?

He wanted to be with her forever, but they also hadn't been dating a very long time. Could a long distance relationship work? Should they just bite the bullet and get engaged now? And, most importantly of all, would Sally even want to relocate?

So many questions swirled through his mind as he and Gramps drove to Sally's for the dinner invitation his aunt had extended for the both of them.

"Kleiner, is everything okay?" his grandfather asked after they'd parked but still hadn't left the car.

Tobias wiped his hands on the legs of his pants and grabbed the door handle. "Just nervous, I guess."

"I already promised I wouldn't say a thing about the cooking," his gramps reminded him. But that was the least of Tobias's worries. Not only would he be meeting Sally's aunt for the first time tonight, but he'd also need to tell them both about the job offer and the fact that he wanted to say yes.

Sally answered the door before they even had the chance to knock. She jumped into Tobias's arms and gave him a giant kiss, which did nothing to ease his nerves. Especially when Gramps made a fake gagging noise.

"Only kidding!" he cried with a chuckle before continuing into the house.

"Tobias," Sally said, pulling him into the kitchen by both hands. Her eyes sparkled with such happiness that he almost forgot his worries about that evening and the news he had yet to share. "This is my aunt Fiona."

"Howdy," Fiona said with a tiny wave before bending down to check on something in the oven. A moment later she trotted up to Sally's side and whispered loud enough for all to hear, "He's a cutie, Sally. Nicely done."

Sally groaned, but Tobias just laughed.

Fiona offered a curt bow to Gramps and said, "We order your food to go all the time. Best in town."

And the old man's face lit brightly at the compliment. "See, *kleiner,* you had nothing to worry about. I love them both already."

The evening passed easily. Everyone enjoyed each other's company with no real hiccups. Sally and Tobias even got a few chances to sneak away and steal kisses when the others weren't looking, and when they were, the two of them held hands beneath the table.

Constantly connected.

A united force.

He hoped that would still be the case after he'd share his big news.

Because, yes, Tobias knew he had to tell Sally and Gramps both about the job offer tonight. It had been eating away at him all day. Maybe now that everyone was fed and happy, it wouldn't be such a big deal. Maybe he had built it up in his mind bigger than it really was.

Deciding to just go for it before he lost the nerve, Tobias clinked the edge of his fork to his water goblet and stood as all eyes turned toward him. "I have an announcement."

He was greeted by a mix of anxious, excited, and questioning expressions. He closed his eyes and hurried on. "Yesterday I got offered a job. A good one. It's in the city, but it's a really good opportunity, and I'm thinking of taking it. I wanted to hear your thoughts before deciding."

"I think you should take it," Sally's aunt said first. "And you should take Sally with you. It could be the perfect opportunity for both of you."

"Aunt Fiona, stop it," Sally hissed, shooting him an embarrassed look.

"What about opening your own firm?" Gramps wanted to know, his thick brows furrowed together in the middle of his forehead.

"I don't know, Gramps. That was more your dream for me than my own. I like the idea of working for someone else, but I'll say no to the job offer if that's what you want."

Okay, maybe he had thought about it more than he'd realized. Because sharing the news with everyone now made him excited. It made him want to say yes to the offer.

"Of course it's not what he wants," Fiona interjected. "He wants what's best for you, period."

Gramps looked as though he were about to become angry, but then he unexpectedly broke into a chuckle. "We only just met, but she's right. I want you to have what you want, *kleiner.*"

"And how about you, Sally?" Tobias asked, noticing his girlfriend had been uncharacteristically silent during this whole exchange. "What do you want?"

NINETEEN

S ally rose from the table slowly. "May I speak to you in private?" she asked Tobias.

He nodded, but his expression instantly fell.

She tried not to think about that as she led him to a quiet corner of the living room. Like her aunt and Tobias's grandfather, she wanted to be excited for him, but this was all so much, so fast. Although she'd never been particularly happy in Sweet Grove, it had been her home for as long as she could remember. Leaving it behind was not a spur of the moment decision. Not like Tobias wanted it to be.

"I need more time," she told him. "This is all happening really fast."

The smile Tobias gave in response was big enough for the both of them. "I know. It was rather unexpected. But so was our finding each other and falling in love. Lately, I've found that the most unexpected parts of my life are what make it the best." He tried so hard to convince her, as if he'd already made up his mind for the both of them.

Sally's stomach twisted into knots. "So you've already decided then?"

"I don't know." His words and demeanor seemed to say entirely different things. "It seems as close to a perfect solution as there can be, given all the balls in the air. But I love you, and I want us to make this decision together."

"But how, Tobias? We haven't been together that long. What if we don't work out?"

Tobias laced his fingers through her and lifted her hands to shoulder height. "Don't say that. Of course we'll work out."

Sally frowned. It wasn't too long ago that she had asked Ben to run away with her on the eve of his wedding. She'd been willing to leave it all behind then, and—now that time had passed—she was so glad now that he'd turned her down. What if her feelings for Tobias also changed with time? She didn't doubt that she loved him, but would that be enough?

"What about my aunt? What about your grandfather? We can't leave them."

Tobias smiled again, but even he must have known it was forced because the grin quickly vanished. "Haven't you seen how well they get along? Maybe they can take care of each other. Plus, we've hired Fred at the restaurant to help manage things for Gramps, and we'll only be a couple hours away. We could come back every weekend if you wanted to." His eyes bore into hers, begging, pleading for her to agree. And she wanted to so badly, but...

"I can't think straight when you look at me like that," she mumbled, biting her lip both to avoid saying more and to discourage him from kissing her.

"What about when I do this?" he asked, bending forward to brush his lips against hers anyway. "Maybe thinking is overrated. Maybe it's time to just feel."

"I don't know what I feel, Tobias. It's such a big decision. I can't make it overnight." If only it were as simple as he wanted it to be. Maybe she was making too big a deal of things, but if she was going to uproot her entire life, then she needed to be certain beyond the shadow of a doubt.

Tobias stroked her cheek delicately. "So you need time to figure things out?"

She nodded and placed her hand on top of his. "I think so."

Tobias smiled again, accepting her terms, whether or not they were ideal for him. "Okay, I can understand that. Should we just relax tomorrow to take the pressure off? Maybe go see a movie or something?"

Sally shook her head, making herself dizzy. "No, I need time... on my own."

His eyes widened, and he wrapped both arms around her, pulling her to his chest. "No, I don't need to take this job. Not if it means there's even the slightest chance of losing you. I can say no. We can stay here forever if you want to."

"That's the thing. I don't know if I want that, either." She hated this. Tobias had always given all of himself to her. Why hadn't she jumped at the chance to do the same? Why couldn't this just be simple?

He rested his forehead on hers and whispered, "Then what are you saying?"

"Give me a week. Seven days. After that, I'll have my answer... about everything."

* * *

Tobias struggled with leaving Sally's house knowing that he wouldn't see her again for at least a week. Not just that, though—she may also choose to end their relationship once the waiting was up. He'd started that day thinking he had it all figured out, that his path was paved toward a future that suited him perfectly.

And now?

He felt like a ghost drifting around Sweet Grove.

Gramps now had Fred to help him with the restaurant, and it didn't make sense for Tobias to work on starting his own firm when he may very well take the job in the city.

Of course, his professor understood and said that she could hold the job offer for a few weeks if he needed her to, but that would be even more waiting, even more torture. He hardly expected to make it through this one week, let alone more.

Everywhere he went around town reminded him of Sally, even the places they hadn't gone together. He could picture her in each setting, smiling in the sunlight, taking her surrounding in silently as the world carried on boisterously around her.

He thought back to their first meeting in the orchard. She'd been flustered, in a hurry. He now knew it was because her heart was breaking, watching Ben marry someone else. Did he feel jealous? *No.* Because he believed Sally when she said she was over Ben. When she said she loved him, Tobias.

But what if love wasn't enough?

What if she simply couldn't escape the life she'd built for herself in Sweet Grove? What if it was too hard? Too scary? Too impossible?

Tobias had thought he and Sally got along because they were so similar, both dealing with the loss of parents, feeling like imposters in their own lives. He realized now, though, that the opposite was true. Despite their similarities, Tobias had always strived to prove himself worthy of the life that had been gifted to him. Sally, on the other hand, only wanted to hide from her greatness. It's what she was doing now. Instead of talking out the possibilities with him, she retreated into herself, asked him to stay away.

It was the same with her writing, even the same with her former crush on Ben. She'd loved him in silence until it was almost too late. She hid in her lonely house with Aunt Fiona. She hid in the quiet library for work. She hid her beautiful imperfection, rarely giving a full-toothed smile.

Why was she so afraid of what she could be? Of what she already was if only she would give herself the chance?

He longed to go to her, to tell her this. And yet…

Tobias knew he needed to respect her wishes and give her the time she'd requested. That left him with only one option.

Tobias prayed.

TWENTY

S ally did whatever she did when she felt lost. She wrote.

Not a letter this time, but rather her novel.

She read over her opening paragraphs:

There once lived a girl with impossibly light skin, a willowy build, and courage that roared through her veins like a mighty river. She grew up believing in fairytales, but now looked back on these childish dreams with consternation. She had no castle, no prince, but she did have more than her fair share of dragons to conquer. And conquer them she would, otherwise what kind of story would this be?

This wasn't the story she had whittled away at for years, but rather a fresh one she'd started after reconnecting with Tobias. Regardless, no matter what she was writing, the heroines were always based on her. She'd yet to finish a story, to find out if these fictional versions of herself really could win in the end.

It was time.

Our tale isn't set in the magical realm. It's here in the real world—in small-town Texas, of all places. It is here our princess waits locked in a high-up tower. This tower, though, isn't made of stonework, and it's not lined with ivy. Her prison is one of her own making. That prison is her walled-off heart.

Sally continued well into the night, removing some paragraphs, adding others, but always, always moving forward. Truth be told, she didn't know how this story would end for her heroine. But she needed to work it out. She had less than seven days remaining to earn a happily ever after for both her and her protagonist.

And like all good stories, this one came complete

with plot twists galore. Sally raced to write the words, to find out what would happen next as she let the heart she had silenced for so long light the way.

This little light of mine…

Too long she'd hidden it away; too long she'd dulled its shine.

She kept the folded up letter she'd written to God on her desk as she worked. She didn't know the way, but He did. He always had. She'd just never thought to ask until now.

"Guide my fingers. Show me my heart," she whispered when she sat down at her keyboard again the next morning.

Six days remained. Six days to figure out what she actually wanted out of this life, not what she thought she needed. Six days to rediscover herself, to revive that little girl she'd hidden deep inside ever since the news of her parents' car crash.

The words flew forth from her fingertips, but the time ticked away just as quickly.

Five days now.

And then four.

She worked through her plot, kept the story moving, eager to see how it would end. Her heroine now thought she'd discovered what she was supposed to be but was so afraid to take the leap.

Three days left.

Sally's wrists ached, her back clenched with pain, and her stomach rumbled from the infrequent meals she'd managed to get in over the past several days. But she didn't care. She needed to finish this. She needed to know.

Two more days to go.

And that was when she knew that she was exactly where she needed to be.

THE END

Impossibly, she'd managed to finish a day early. Finally, she knew. She had the answer she'd been so desperately seeking, and now it was time to share it with Tobias.

She only hoped he would understand.

A gentle rapping sounded on Tobias's front door. Could it be Sally coming to give her answer?

He raced to answer, but found his porch step empty. That is, until he looked down and spotted a thick manila envelope with his name scrawled across the front. He stooped to collect it and pried the metal fastener open. A few stark words stood out in the center of the mostly blank cover page.

THE STORY OF A LIFE ALMOST LIVED
by Sally Scott

Then she'd done it! She'd finished her book, and now she wanted him to read it. Tobias wished Sally was here with him, wished he could hug her and tell her how proud he was of her.

But he knew he was meant to read now, that he would find his answer among the pages. And so he sat down, right there on the porch step, and turned the page.

This book is for anyone who's ever felt unloved, unwanted, or un-anything. Life isn't meant to be almost lived.

His heart fluttered as he turned the next page. Did this mean she'd decided to leave Sweet Grove with him? Did this mean they could be together, start a new life side by side?

He turned the page again, quickly becoming

immersed in the story. Sally had told him she wrote fantasy romance, but this story was grounded in the real world. Their world. He recognized scenes from their time together as well as fictionalized versions of memories Sally had shared, and he knew that this was more than just a book to her.

It held her answers to everything.

But more than anything, he needed to know what she'd chosen when it came to him.

Would she keep on loving him forever? Or had encouraging her to find herself result in her finding a better way forward… a way without him?

He kept reading, laughing in some places, fighting back tears in others. The sun faded from the sky and he could barely see the words before him on the page, but still he read. And at last by the light of the stars, he finished:

And that was when she knew that she was exactly where she needed to be.

Although Sally had typed THE END, there was still one more page inside the envelope. He picked up the entire bundle and carried it inside with him, instinctively knowing that these words would be the most important of all.

Gramps sat at the table working on a puzzle. When Tobias entered, he asked, "Where have you been all day? What's that you've got there?"

But Tobias shushed him, needing nothing but the remaining words. Sally's final words that would close out the story.

He turned his back, not caring if his grandfather chose to read over his shoulder—just so long as he was able to absorb the words, to find out what Sally needed with this one last page.

This is my first novel, but I know it won't be the last. You see, life gives us many stories, and this is just one that I needed to tell. A wise author once told me that the first book is the most important, that it's the one tale that most needs to get out there in the world. Well, she was definitely right about that!

For a long time, I didn't know what I wanted. As the title of this book suggests, I was merely almost living. I thought I had a pretty good idea of what it would take to make me happy but somehow always missed the mark.

Actually, scratch that. I know exactly how I

missed it each time. I never aimed for the bullseye.

I intentionally went after targets I knew I couldn't hit. My quiet job in a small town had no opportunities for growth but it allowed me to write. Unfortunately, those stories had no real conflict, or even endings. I fell in love with someone I deep down knew could never love me back. I used my aunt's illness as a reason not to spread my wings and venture out from the nest.

Everything I did was done with the subconscious goal of achieving mediocrity. My life was almost good, but never quite got there.

Until...

Until I met someone who wouldn't take good enough for an answer.

Until I met someone who'd also been dealt a tough lot but used that as motivation to shine.

Until I found my forever in the form of a man I hadn't been brave enough to dream.

Until you opened up my heart and stepped inside, made a home.

I love you, Tobias, and I will follow you anywhere.

Let's shine together.

Let's live life all the way.

Tobias clutched that last page to his chest, a smile stretching from one corner of his face to the other. Ignoring his grandfather's many questions, he bolted out the door and drove straight to Sally's house.

She, too, sat outside on the porch, waiting. When he slammed the car door shut, she rose, a shy smile on her face. "Did you read it?"

"Every last page. I especially liked that last page, by the way." He picked her up off her feet and hugged her tight before bringing his mouth to hers in their first kiss after what had felt like a lifetime apart.

But there was one thing Tobias needed to know. "Why did you end the story one way, but then say something else in your letter to me?"

She looked up at him from beneath long eyelashes. "Remember that poem we all had to read in high school? Robert Frost? 'The Road Less Taken?'"

Tobias nodded, understanding now. "You wanted to see how the other choice would play out. What did you find?"

She hugged him harder, and he never wanted her to let him go. "That I'd be miserable without you. You're the first person to ever make me want more, to believe I could have more."

"And what do you want?" he asked, needing to hear the words aloud this time.

"Tobias, I just want you." A mischievous smile crept across her face, visible even by the pale light of the moon. "And maybe a kitten?"

EPILOGUE

TWO MONTHS LATER

S ally gave Jet one more scratch behind his tiny ears before grabbing her satchel and heading out the door. As promised, Tobias had given her a sweet black kitten as a housewarming gift when she'd at last made the big move to Houston.

He'd gone ahead of her a couple weeks earlier to secure leases for both of them. Even though they weren't living together yet, they had managed to get units in the same building and already had plans to move into a larger unit together after their wedding the following spring.

For now, though, Sally liked having her own space. It was the first time she'd ever lived by herself —well, other than Jet—and she found it quite relaxing. It was also the perfect place to work on her next novel.

MC Raven had come through as promised and shared Sally's completed manuscript with her own agent. The agent wasted no time in getting back to Sally and asking if she could turn her one book into a three-book series. He said he knew for sure New York would come calling in no time and that they'd demand more, more, more.

Speaking of MC Raven, she and Sally had become good friends. Each week they would meet up in either Sally's apartment or MC's house for a friendly, albeit somewhat competitive, write-in. They also brought their kittens so the feisty little felines could have a playdate of their own.

Sally kept her promise to MC, too. After Tobias proposed, she wasted no time in asking her favorite author turned good friend if she would serve as the matron of honor for her wedding. MC cried actual tears of joy when she accepted.

After all those years of wondering whether her real life waited for her outside of the tiny town of Sweet Grove, Sally had found her answer.

A resounding yes!

Sure, Houston wasn't exactly New York, Paris, or Sydney, but it was the place she and Tobias had elected to build their futures together. She loved the abundance of choices the big city provided for food, entertainment, friends, everything. The only thing missing was Aunt Fiona.

Luckily, they were able to make the drive to Sweet Grove most weekends to check in on things in their hometown. Aunt Fiona had started a new regimen of medications and had doubled up on her talk therapy. It seemed to be helping, but what was helping even more was the friendship she'd formed with Tobias's grandfather, of all people.

The old man often cut out of work early to stop by Fiona's house and spend the evenings with her. They cooked, listened to audiobooks, Facetimed Sally and Tobias, and just generally enjoyed each other's company. Neither was looking for love, which made them perfect for each other. And so their deep friendship grew, making the special new family that consisted of the four of them even stronger.

Sally smiled to herself as she pulled open the heavy doors of the Houston Public Library. She did that a lot these days—smiled. She didn't even try to hide the gap between her two front teeth that had once embarrassed her like nothing else could. Now she embraced her uniqueness, because it was what made her memorable.

Besides, Tobias said he loved it.

"Hi," she said to the woman at the checkout

counter. "I'm here to interview for the part-time staff position."

The woman smiled and gestured for Sally to follow her to the back. "Yes, right this way."

Although Tobias made good money at his new job, Sally knew she would always want to work. Her calling was to bring good stories to others, stories that could help them. Not just her own, of course, but to share the great works written by the thousands of brilliant souls that had come before her.

That passion was her light in the world.

And—by golly—she was going to let it shine.

AFTERWORD

Both Tobias and Sally had a lot to prove—to themselves, to each other, to the world at large. Too many people in their lives had told them they weren't enough. And they'd internalized these words, allowing them to become enormous roadblocks to achieving their dreams.

When you live with low self-esteem, it's easy to cling to what's known... even when what's known isn't good for you and may even be hurting you. What if it's too big, too scary, *too much* for little old me? Sometimes it's easier to hide, to deprive ourselves of life's greatest victories with the hopes of also avoiding life's greatest battles.

So then how can you prove yourself when you avoid any real opportunities to do so?

Tobias and Sally are very much alike in this way, as is Sally's Aunt Fiona.

As once was I.

Ahh, who am I kidding? Often, *still*, so am I.

Friends are so crucial to overcoming self-constructed barriers. Not just any friends, though. We all need someone to believe in us and work on getting us to believe in ourselves while they're at it. Tobias did that for Sally.

My friend Mallory—to whom this book is dedicated—does that for me.

I am blessed with an amazing support system in my life: a wonderful, loving husband; a sweet, creative daughter; five dogs, an extended family who loves me; a wealth of online friends; and amazing readers. They make so many things possible to me.

But it wasn't until I formed my friendship with Mallory that I really began to challenge myself. I remember being so nervous and not wanting to make a new friend, constantly wondering what she must be thinking of me, feeling embarrassed about my appearance or fearful that I would say the wrong thing...

She was very patient and understanding with me, though, and our friendship grew and grew. Now she encourages me to go all kinds of places, like out-of-state (out-of-country even!) writer conferences, concerts, you name it.

It's easier to believe in myself, knowing that she believes in me and that if things get awkward or hard, she'll already be there to support me.

Still… every time we do something big and new, I get so anxious and debate canceling. Yes, every time I end up going anyway and am always so glad I did!

In *Love's Trial*, Sally reflects that comparison is the thief of joy, but anxiety can rob you of your happiness as well. So, yes, it was easy for me to write Aunt Fiona's character because I, too, suffer from an anxiety so strong I have a hard time leaving the house. I also haven't driven in years because of this same anxiety.

But the people who love me keep at me, keep me from retreating too far into myself or my anxiety.

The thing about trials is that we don't have to face them on our own. There is always a choice. For the longest time, I shut people out of my life, people who wanted to be there, for fear that I wasn't good enough, that I didn't deserve them.

It was only when I began to reopen those doors that I learned what was truly possible.

Life itself is a trial, but we don't need to go it alone. Reach for friends, family, God. Reach for each other.

And soon you'll find that anything is possible.

ACKNOWLEDGMENTS

Every book is a new labor of love, and *Love's Trial* was no exception!

This time I'd like to pay special thanks to my best writing buddy, Mallory Crowe. Not only did she serve as partial inspiration for Sally's character—down to the long dark hair and shared gap between their front teeth—but she was the basis for Sally's idol MC Raven as well!

Often, we have everything we need to be our own heroes. You don't need a cape or a secret identity—just believe in yourself. Mallory, you can do and be anything. Keep choosing *fabulous* every single day. Remember, the things Sally least liked about herself were the ones Tobias ultimately loved most.

Also, dear readers, if you enjoy romances with a little bit of steam, then check out Mallory Crowe's books and meet great characters between the pages as well as the great character behind the pen. I can't recommend Mallory as an author—or as a person—quite enough!

You see, without her, I'd very much be like Aunt Fiona, hiding inside my house afraid to venture out in the world. I complain that she makes me get out and do things but am ultimately very grateful she serves as a bridge between my anxiety and ability to get out there and enjoy life.

I hope you are also blessed with friends who accept you as you are but also lovingly encourage you to be even better, to grow, to learn… to live.

Thanks also goes to the many others who help me live my best life by writing stories like Sally's and Tobias's.

To my husband, Falcon.

Daughter, Phoenix.

To my parents, brothers, sisters, nieces, nephews, cousins, aunts, uncles, and every other relation under the sun.

My life saver, Angi.

Team of friends and book experts, Mallory (yes, another one!), Megan, and Jasmine.

To the thousands of readers who have given one of my books a home on your eReader, who have written me messages of encouragement, who have reached out and become new and very much appreciated friends.

To Becky, Ines, and all the authors I regularly procrastinate with when we should all be writing! Sometimes procrastinating is the most inspiring part of the entire process, you know.

And of course my five dogs must also be thanked for their assistance in completing this book, especially my sweet Chihuahua girl, Sky Princess, who cuddled beside me as I wrote each and every word.

She and I both hope you enjoyed the story!

GET TEXT UPDATES

Well, here's something cool... You can now sign up to get text notifications for all my most important book news. You can choose to receive them for New Releases, New Pre-Orders, or Special Sales--or any combination of the three.

These updates will be short, sweet, and to the point with a link to the new book or deal on your favorite retailer.

You choose when you receive them, making this new way of communicating fully customized to your needs as a reader.

Sign up at www.MelStorm.com/TextMe

* * *

The First Street Church Romances

Sweet and wholesome small town love stories with the community church at their center make for the perfect feel-good reads!

Love's Prayer

Love's Promise

Love's Prophet

Love's Vow

Love's Trial

Love's Treasure

Love's Testament

Love's Gift

* * *

The Alaska Sunrise Romances

These quick, light-hearted romances will put a smile on your face and a song in your heart. It's time to indulge in a sweet Alaskan get-away!

Must Love Music

Must Love Military

Must Love Mistletoe

Must Love Mutts

Must Love Mommy

Must Love Moo

Must Love Mustangs

Must Love Miracles

Must Love Mermaids

Must Love Movie Star

* * *

The Church Dogs of Charleston

A very special litter of Chihuahua puppies born on Christmas day is adopted by the local church and immediately set to work as tiny therapy dogs.

Little Loves

Mini Miracles

Dainty Darlings

Tiny Treasures

* * *

The Memory Ranch Romances

This new Sled Dogs-spinoff series harnesses the restorative power of both horses and love at Elizabeth Jane's therapeutic memory ranch.

Memories of Home

Memories of Heaven

Memories of Healing

* * *

The Finding Mr. Happily Ever After Series

One bride, four possible grooms, unlimited potential for disaster to strike. Is the man waiting at the end of the aisle the one that's meant to be Jazz's forever love?

Nathan

Chase

Xavier

Edwin

The Finale

* * *

Stand-Alone Novels and Novellas

Whether climbing ladders in the corporate world or taking care of things at home, every woman has a story to tell.

Angels in Our Lives

A Mother's Love

A Colorful Life

* * *

Special Collections & Boxed Sets

From light-hearted comedies to stories about finding hope in the darkest of times, these special boxed editions offer a great way to catch up or to fall in love with Melissa Storm's books for the first time.

Small Town Beginnings: A Series Starter Set

The Sled Dog Series: Books 1-5

The First Street Church Romances: Books 1-3

The Alaska Sunrise Romances: Books 1-5

Finding Mr. Happily Ever After: Books 1-5

True Love Eternal: The 1950's Collection

ABOUT THE AUTHOR

Melissa Storm is a mother first, and everything else second. Writing is her way of showing her daughter just how beautiful life can be, when you pay attention to the everyday wonders that surround us. So, of course, Melissa's USA Today bestselling fiction is highly personal and often based on true stories.

Melissa loves books so much, she married fellow author Falcon Storm. Between the two of them, there are always plenty of imaginative, awe-inspiring stories to share. Melissa and Falcon also run a number of book-related businesses together, including LitRing, Sweet Promise Press, Novel Publicity, Your Author Engine, and the Author Site. When she's not reading, writing, or child-rearing, Melissa spends time relaxing at home in the company of a seemingly unending quantity of dogs and a rescue cat named Schrödinger.

GET IN TOUCH!
www.MelStorm.com
author@melstorm.com

33069442R00134

Made in the USA
Columbia, SC
07 November 2018